Branded But
BROKE

The Journey Begins

L.A. LOGAN

 DonJay Publishing

Branded But Broke – The Journey Begins

Editing by Karen Rodgers

Cover and book design by Rebecca Hayes

Published in the United States by
DonJay Publishing
P O Box 442
Little Rock, AR 72203

ISBN 978-0-578-44313-3

LCCN 2019930503

Other books by L. A. Logan –

This book is dedicated to anyone who thought fame, fortune and material things could buy your happiness.

True happiness starts within. Matthew 16:26

The teachers and administrators at William Hall High Charter School in Austin, Texas have more love triangles going than the students they were hired to teach. With each secret affair that's discovered, it becomes apparent that each employee has a taste for the finer things in life and most are willing to do whatever it takes to obtain it.

But under the name brand tags are many broken pieces that refuse to be held together by material things. Each has a story to tell…

The Ladies

L. A. Logan

Naylor

ONE

It was Monday morning and Naylor was inching in and out of the slow traffic on the I-35 in an effort to get to work on time. She should've been there at that very moment, instead of glaring at each driver that refused to let her merge in front of them, but instead she'd chosen to take those extra thirty minutes with Donavon, knowing she didn't have them to spare.

This would be her fourth time running late in the past two weeks and she knew Whitney Maxton, her boss, wasn't going to be happy with her. She decided to stop fighting with traffic and save all her energy for the *talk* she knew Whitney would be having with her before the day was out.

"I've got to stop this nonsense. If the church mothers could see me now," Naylor said out loud, gently hitting her palm on her wood-grained steering wheel.

As her music blared in the background, Naylor was not so much frustrated with the traffic, but more so with herself. She knew her nonchalant attitude and behavior needed to change, especially since it was starting to affect her job.

Although her job was technically fifteen minutes away, in heavy traffic, it could easily turn into forty-five minutes. Austin, TX morning traffic was now at a dead stop and

Naylor was even more frustrated as she could see exit 232A a few feet in front of her. She waited a few minutes before deciding that getting a ticket for driving on the shoulder was worth the risk if it bought her at least five more minutes of time. As soon as she reached her exit, her cell phone rang. She already knew who it was.

"Hello?" Naylor said, rolling her eyes in annoyance.

"Where are you? I told you I wanted you to show the new English teacher's aide around! Candice is out on maternity leave and I didn't want her substitute handling it," Naylor heard Whitney say.

"I know, I know, I know. I wasn't feeling too well this morning and almost called in but realized I promised to help out," Naylor said, driving 30 mph through the employee parking lot instead of the posted 10 mph.

She had caught a break in the traffic along with running a couple of red lights.

"Okay, so, can you answer my original question please?" Whitney asked, irritation evident in her tone.

"I'm in the teachers' lounge. Where is she?" Naylor asked, shuffling down the hall towards the office.

She was doing her best not to sound out of breath after the sprint she had made from the car to the lounge and now towards the main office.

"You mean where is *he* and his name is Eddie. He is in the office waiting on you to show up," Whitney said, growing more frustrated.

"Okay, I must have misheard you, I thought you said the name was Edith. I'm coming through the office door now," Naylor said, before hanging up.

Naylor stood outside in the hallway for a few more moments in an effort to catch her breath. There was no way she wanted Whitney to know just how late she was really running.

Naylor Jones was a 9th grade English teacher at William Hall High Charter School and had been there since its inception six years ago. She and Whitney had started at the school at the same time as the teachers, but Whitney was recently promoted to principal. Naylor was struggling to adjust to this change, mainly because Whitney had become one of her best friends throughout the past six years. Naylor was also secretly jealous that Whitney was promoted over her. Although she and Whitney had the same experience, Naylor felt her degree should have sealed the job for her, not for her best friend.

Naylor was doing her best to keep her true feelings under wraps since their council board members recently approved adding two assistant principal positions due to the increasing attendance at the school. She was sure as long as she acted accordingly she would be the number one pick for one of the two positions.

"There she is! Eddie, this is Naylor. Naylor, meet Eddie," Naylor heard Whitney's obnoxious voice say as soon as she entered the office.

Naylor, originally distracted by all the kids and parents that were in the office, hadn't noticed Whitney or her new co-worker until she heard her name from the left of the room. She wondered how she had put up with Whitney's voice for all these years or if maybe, her voice had only become nerve-racking because she was now her boss.

"Well hello, Naylor. It's nice to meet you," Eddie said, extending his hand for a handshake.

Naylor was slightly speechless at the sight that was before her. He wasn't bad looking by her standards—a little short for her taste—but still doable. Eddie looked like he

5

stood 5'10"and weighed around 250lbs, give or take 10lbs. His skin was flawless, the color of night at its darkest moment. He was beautiful, but not in a metro sexual kind of way, but in a manly man way.

Before she started to undress him with her eyes, Naylor was distracted once again by that annoying voice.

"Naylor? Are you okay?" she heard Whitney ask.

"Yes, I'm fine. I'm sorry Eddie, you look familiar to me, and I was trying to figure out why. Anyway, give me a little time and it will come to me. It is nice to meet you. Are you ready to get your first day on the job started?" Naylor asked, purposely ignoring Whitney.

"No problem. I'm ready when you are," Eddie said, smiling.

Naylor thought she would faint at the sight of those pretty pearly white teeth. She had to really talk to herself because she felt her mind trying to take her to a thought that had no business taking place in a school. The one thing she was going to do was look up his Facebook profile to see what his relationship status was. Depending on what she saw, she just might have to give somebody a run for their money.

"Eddie, Naylor will take great care of you, but if you need anything, don't hesitate to contact me. Again, welcome to the team," Naylor heard Whitney talking as she was doing her best to get him out of the office.

Naylor was going to do everything within her power to make sure Eddie would never trust Whitney, even if she had to tell a couple of white lies to accomplish it.

TWO

Naylor Jones was a man's dreamy secret and a woman's worst nightmare. She stood 5'0" tall, weighing 115lbs with off-black Indian Remy hair with large barrel curls resting below her shoulders. She was a woman that had not met a line she wasn't willing to cross if it meant getting what she wanted. As far as she was concerned the world was hers and everyone that was in her world had to conform to how she wanted things to be. If they didn't, she would stop at nothing to make life uncomfortable all while being their best friend.

Regardless of her current circumstances, she had big dreams and that coupled with her "by any means necessary" attitude made her a very dangerous woman. She wanted what she wanted, when she wanted, and it didn't matter who she had to throw under the bus to get it.

"Are you hungry?" Naylor asked Eddie as they made their way into the teachers' lounge.

"Yes indeed. I'm surprised you didn't hear my stomach talking during the last two periods. I had a small breakfast this morning and my appetite isn't used to that. What are you having for lunch?" Eddie asked, holding his hand over his stomach.

They had made it to their destination and Naylor watched him as he warmed his spaghetti in the black microwave. She liked what she saw. He was dressed in dark blue slacks and a light and dark blue-checkered button down Ralph Lauren shirt.

"I'm having a salad, but you better watch out. I just might take your lunch and make you eat this salad," Naylor answered, holding a fork full of lettuce up in the air.

Eddie laughed showing those pearly whites once more. Naylor smiled at the vision before her. If only he knew the thoughts that were running rampant in her mind.

"So, where are you from?" Naylor asked Eddie once he was comfortable in his seat.

"I'm from Dallas. The Ft. Worth area," Eddie said, taking a bite of his food before continuing.

"I moved down here with my cousin. We both wanted something a little slower paced than Dallas, so we packed up and came to Austin. It's been cool so far," Eddie explained.

As Naylor sat there listening to him talk, she had to ask herself why she was so fascinated with this man. The more he talked, the more relaxed he became, and she could tell he was far from a choir boy, which was right up her alley. This made her even more curious about him.

Again, Naylor had to ask herself why she was allowing him to gain her attention with each word he spoke. It wasn't like she was in need of a boyfriend or male companionship. She already had three men on the line and she really didn't want to fit another one in unless he could heavily contribute to the Naylor Fund.

Anybody who knew Naylor knew she lived above her means. She was a walking and talking name brand contradiction on a $47,000 a year teacher's salary. She drove a fully loaded Toyota Avalon and lived in one of the more expensive areas of Austin. The rent on her two-bedroom townhouse was $1100 a month and she was responsible for all utilities. To say Naylor was addicted to shopping would be a tremendous understatement. She lived and breathed for clothes, shoes, jewelry, handbags and they all had to be name brand.

Naylor made no apologies for her attitude, her spending habits and how she afforded the things she had become accustomed to. As far as she was concerned she was entitled to these things, simply because she wanted them. Everyone could have what she had if they weren't so stuck in the *independent woman* mindset that Destiny's Child got started. She did consider herself independent but that didn't stop her from strategically seeking out men she knew could give her what she wanted at her command. It also didn't stop her from ending things without a second thought the minute they couldn't or wouldn't give her what she wanted.

Donavon, the man who made her knees buckle the night before, would be her ideal man if she was ready to settle down. He worked for a large Internet company that had him out of town four days out the week, sometimes more. They seemed to be on the same page, both said they didn't want anything heavy at this point in their lives, just companionship.

Donavon paid her $600.00 a month car payment and half of her rent. That's why she'd had to give him those extra thirty minutes this morning, plus she loved the way he made her feel. Naylor had him under the impression that the $600.00 included her insurance payment each month, when in reality it did not. Her car note was high because of her poor credit score, which was due to her poor life choices. If she had to choose between paying her bills on time and

9

catching a sale at the mall, her bills would have to take a back seat—several seats if the sale was real good.

There were times when it wasn't all about the money. Naylor had been known to date a man for pure physical pleasure. Whenever she did have a Naylor Toy in the mix, she treated them how she saw them. They dare not contact her first and she made it very clear which lane they were in and to stay in it unless she said otherwise. She was the one to initiate contact and if they didn't like it, she would deactivate their Naylor Passport and dispose of them like a potential spy who entered the country illegally. Now when it came to Eddie, she was still on the fence as to what lane, if any, he would be in.

"Are you from here, Naylor?" Eddie asked, taking a drink from his flavored Vitamin water.

"No, I'm originally from Iowa. I went to school at TSU in Houston and fell in love with Texas. Of course my family wanted me to find a job closer to home, but I wasn't about that life anymore. Texas had made me into a new woman," Naylor said with a slight chuckle while taking a small bite of her salad.

"What made you fall in love with Texas?" Eddie asked, wiping his mouth with his napkin.

Naylor wasn't sure if he was trying to secretly seduce her or what. If he was, it was working.

"It wasn't Iowa, that's what! Come on, we've got to get back to our class," Naylor said, laughing and getting up from the table.

The last thing she wanted to do was let him know his charm was breaking her down.

10

THREE

It was 3:45 p.m., thirty minutes since school had dismissed for the day and fifteen minutes since Naylor had watched Eddie walk to his car from her classroom window. That walk was an intriguing sight and a relaxing way to end a day that started out very hectic. Before she had laid eyes on Eddie, her hope was for the day to end before it had even started. After meeting and spending the entire workday with him, she didn't want it to end. That feeling did confuse her, especially since Eddie was a couple pay grades beneath her.

After Eddie was in his car, Naylor began to pack up her things to head home for an early dinner at the expense of Craig and happy she had dodged another god-forsaken meeting with Whitney. Her day had ended on a good note and she didn't want to ruin it by dealing with her used-to-be best friend. Just as she was heading out her classroom door, Whitney was walking through it.

I just had to watch that man walk to his car, Naylor thought to herself.

"Hey, Whitney, you have plans after you leave here?" Naylor asked, purposely sounding personal.

"No, not today, I have a board meeting to attend this evening," Whitney answered, now taking a seat at the student desk that was directly in front of Naylor's desk.

Naylor walked over to her desk while willing her mind to stay focused. She knew Whitney had purposely come down to her classroom at this particular time. Even the staff that barely knew Naylor knew she made it her business to be out of the school no later than thirty minutes after class let out. Naylor figured this was just another one of Whitney's ways of reminding her she was the boss and could make her stay as late as she wanted to.

Before she became principal, Whitney would go with Naylor to the Night Life Lounge for a no-holds-barred Monday night on the town. The two often times got into things they dared not share with anyone else; things that solidified their friendship, their sisterhood. At the time they were both church girls who were going out of their way to shed the holy roller image that had followed them since high school. Those days of friendship and being regular attendees at the church house had become almost non-existent.

Once Naylor reached her desk, she chose not to sit, but stand; this was her way of reminding Whitney she didn't have time for a long lecture.

"Naylor what's going on with you?" Whitney asked.

Naylor struggled to keep calm, mainly because she felt Whitney was out of line for asking her that question. After all, she wasn't the one who had changed. She was the only one who had remained true between the two of them. The more Naylor thought about this, the more she boiled on the inside. She'd had just about enough of this brand new Whitney.

"Nothing is going on with me. What's going on with you?" Naylor responded, a hint of an attitude rolled off her tongue.

Whitney got up and walked over to close the door to the classroom. This made Naylor even more irritated. She didn't have time for Principal Whitney and was ready to let her know the minute Whitney pushed the wrong button.

"I thought you told me you wanted to be the next assistant principal," Whitney said, walking back to take her seat.

"I do!" Naylor said in an elevated tone with attitude on her tongue.

"Do you think you're doing all you can to make that happen?" Whitney asked, looking Naylor in the eye.

"I do!" Naylor responded, with a clear attitude.

Whitney paused before she spoke and this caused Naylor to shift her weight from right to left.

"Look, Naylor, the board asked my opinion about you possibly being promoted. I honestly don't think you're ready. I know that we are friends outside of work, but there is a difference between business and personal. I will not recommend you to the board just because we're friends. I need to know that you've truly changed so that you can handle the responsibility that comes along with the promotion," Whitney explained, disappointment in her voice.

"So, you're better than me now? Have you forgotten what we—you and I—used to do before you were promoted? Now you want to throw it up in my face like you have been so perfect, Whitney?" Naylor said, no professionalism in her voice.

"You see, that's what I am talking about. I keep telling you over and over again this has nothing to do with our

13

friendship. This is about us growing up. We are pushing thirty and it's past time we start acting our age. What we did back in the day when we didn't know better is just that, back in the day; it shouldn't still be our present-day mindset," Whitney said, not as professional as she'd started out.

"So what are you saying, Whitney? Are you saying you're the only one who has got their stuff together and I'm still trying to get there?" Naylor said, now standing from the desk with her left hand on her hip.

Whitney stood to adjust her black pin-striped pants suit, a sign the conversation was coming to an end.

"What I'm saying is if you want to be promoted and taken seriously, you can't keep doing the same things we were doing three plus years ago, Naylor. Let's start with baby steps. First things first, you need to do whatever it takes in order for you to get to work on time. Let's start there before we can even think about putting you in charge of adults who *do* come to work on time and *do* take their jobs very seriously," Whitney said before walking out the door.

Naylor was furious and knew she had to leave the building now before she said or did something that would cost her the paycheck she already had spent. She gathered her things in haste and managed to drop several of her students' assignments in the process. Once Naylor had successfully gathered everything, she made her way to the door and prayed she wouldn't bump into Whitney. If she did, there would be no controlling her actions and she would be in the unemployment line first thing in the morning.

As she walked down the hallway she could hear the bottoms of her Rachel Roy's echoing in the hall. When she reached the front door she heard Brazil, one of her latest work besties, call her name.

"Hey girl, what's up?" Naylor heard Brazil ask.

Naylor was tempted to ignore Brazil to prevent her from being the receiver of the pent-up frustration that was meant for Whitney. She decided to acknowledge her since she was one of the last Mohicans she had in the friends department. Her list was growing shorter by the day.

"Hey lady, getting ready to do my usual. What's up with you?" Naylor asked.

Naylor purposely put the bait out there. After the way her day had just ended, Naylor really didn't feel like going to Night Life alone. She needed to see Craig in order to get the money for her utilities and groceries for the week, but she was not in the mood to pay him for his services, mainly because she was still tired from dealing with Donavon. If she didn't already have her entire check allocated for credit card payments and Dillard's upcoming semi annual sale, she would cancel on him. She was hoping he was in a good mood because she had been eyeing a $650 Michael Kors purse and matching wallet and she was $300 short from getting it.

"Oh, can I ride out with you? After the day I had, I need a little something to change my mood," Brazil said, excitement in her voice.

Gotcha! Naylor thought to herself. It was amazing how well she knew her friends and what buttons to push in order to get what she wanted out of them.

"Girl, of course. You want to meet me there or ride together?" Naylor asked, as the two walked out the door.

"We can take my car if you want," Brazil offered.

Naylor was glad Brazil offered to drive because that would save on her gas and Brazil usually wanted to leave early. This would mean more money in Naylor's pocket and it would be her way of escape from Craig. There was no way

Craig would make her stay until he closed the lounge knowing she had to go to work the next morning.

Craig Spencer, or Spence as his friends called him, was Naylor's ride or die guy. No matter what she needed, he always had her back. It had been this way for the past eight years. When she met him she had just graduated from college and was working as a substitute teacher at Logan Junior High. He was a part-time football coach who worked overtime to get her attention.

Initially she wasn't attracted to him but the more they talked, the more she liked him as a person. As their friendship grew, he started helping her financially and eventually their relationship turned physical. The one thing she loved about Craig was he played his position well. They never had a falling out about what the other may or may not be doing and she liked it like that.

After putting her things in her own car, Naylor jumped into Brazil's Honda Civic and put her seatbelt on. If Naylor had her way, she would much prefer to hang out with Whitney instead of Brazil, but based on how things were going between her and Whitney that would most likely never happen.

Brazil had only been teaching at the school the past two years and was still young and wet behind the ears. In a lot of ways she reminded Naylor of herself and with a little grooming she might be her protégée. The one thing about Brazil Naylor couldn't stand was her lack of ability to control her attitude once she started drinking. If she had one too many drinks and the wrong thing happened to set her off, she would get them put out. The only reason they had never been put out of the Night Life was because of Craig.

"Now, don't start nothing tonight, Brazil. I'm dressed too cute for you to go hood on me this evening. Okay?" Naylor said as she fixed her hair in the mirror.

"Girl, I told you I'm outgrowing that foolishness. I'm about getting my money. I dare not let one of these unemployed females get me off my square, best believe that," Brazil said, applying lip-gloss in between words.

"Cool, let's go in here have a few drinks, get a few numbers and go home with the same amount of money or more than we walked in here with!" Naylor said, laughing as she got out the car.

L. A. Logan

FOUR

Naylor walked in the lounge and commanded the room's attention, purposely making Brazil feel and look like a cheap invitation of her. Her Miss Me Jeans were hugging her in all the right places and her peach V-neck top, complemented by teal accessories, showed the right amount of cleavage without looking easy. Her six-inch peach and teal Rachel Roy's gave her just enough height to make her small frame stand out.

Naylor enjoyed secretly making anybody she hung out with feel inadequate when they were around her. She never wanted them to think for one minute they were on the same level as she was. The only person this egotistical behavior didn't work on was Whitney. No matter what Naylor tried to pull, Whitney was always on point and confident within herself.

Secretly this always annoyed Naylor but also made her more competitive. Whitney always told her it wasn't a competition because they were friends and friends don't compete with each other. She remembered the first time Whitney told her that. It was right after Naylor secretly purchased the same pair of shoes Whitney had a few weeks prior. Naylor made sure she wore her shoes first to make it appear Whitney was trying to be like her.

"Why do you keep doing that?" Naylor remembered Whitney asking.

"What do I keep doing?" Naylor responded, looking clueless.

"Every time we go shopping together, you take note of everything I buy. Then you go and purchase the same things and wear them before I've had a chance to wear mine," Whitney explained, clearly perturbed.

"Whitney, are you serious, right now? It's just a pair of shoes and you couldn't have possibly thought they stopped making them after you purchased your pair," Naylor said, chuckling as if Whitney was really joking.

"Naylor, I know it's a pair of shoes and yes, I know they didn't stop making them after I purchased mine. What I don't know and understand is if your purchases are truly innocent. Why don't you ever tell me you've purchased them?" Whitney explained, no joking in her tone.

"Come on, Whitney, tell me you're not afraid of a little competition," Naylor responded, sounding as if she was joking but secretly enjoying the aggravation that was apparent on Whitney's face.

"When are you going to stop this nonsense? There is no competition between *true* friends. When I loan you money to pay your bills because you've run short on your bills that month, I help because I'm *truly* your friend. When I run short and you help me, you view it as competition and something you can use to down talk me," Whitney explained, aggravation turning into hurt.

Naylor remembered the two of them going back and forth until they agreed to disagree. This blow up happened six months ago and Naylor wondered if the reason Whitney started to turn on her back then was because she had inside information on the position she was promoted to. The position Naylor felt belonged to her and her so-called friend stole right from under her.

Shortly after Naylor and Brazil took their seats, the waitress appeared at their table right on cue. The two ladies ordered a glass of wine before heading over to the buffet full of any type of food a person attending happy hour could want. Both ladies fixed small plates and headed back over to their table.

As they made small talk, it was almost time for the live band's performance. Naylor saw Jay Holmes and his band members taking the stage and a mischievous smile crept across her face. Jay was one sexy man and his stage presence was nostalgic. It reminded Naylor of their last rendezvous. When Jay was finished filling her body with unimaginable pleasure one night after the lounge closed, she felt like she had suffocated, even with all the air that was around her. He had her head swimming with confused emotions and thoughts. She wanted Jay to be a regular on Team Naylor, but he refused her, something about him being best friends with Craig was getting in the way.

When the band began to sing, Naylor saw Craig behind the bar. When he made eye contact, a smile came across his face. She knew he truly loved her along with all her faults and would do anything for her, but she couldn't see herself settling down with him. Naylor had asked herself a thousand times, why she could not bring herself to settle down with Craig and she kept coming up with superficial reasons that wouldn't matter to the average person.

Craig was 6'3" tall and weighed over 280 lbs and appeared to be a loveable teddy bear. He had a very sweet personality, knew how to treat a woman, and despite his weight challenges, was a great lover. He recently lost 30 lbs after joining a boot camp at Naylor's insistence. She told Craig he was getting too old to have so much weight on him. When he showed some resistance, she played the one card that always worked.

"Don't you want to have kids one day and be around to see them grow up?" she remembered saying to him.

Naylor did her best not to use that card very often but wasn't afraid to pull it out when it worked in her favor. Craig was five years older than Naylor and had been married once before. The marriage didn't produce any children, the one thing he wanted but had not accomplished. She was surprised nobody had slipped one in on him yet, as he would be an awesome father and provider. His child or the mother for that matter would never want for anything.

Craig was once a professional football player and had played for three different NFL teams before he retired. Between his savings from his football career, his retirement plan and the money from his nightclub, Craig didn't have to work for the school district, but his love for kids couldn't keep him away. He worked as a school counselor and football coach at Silver Lake High, considered one of the high-risk schools in Austin; he felt it was his duty to help the kids at that school. He felt like that was his way of giving back, along with the many charity events held throughout the year.

"Hey, you. When did you slip in on me?" Craig asked, hugging Naylor as soon as she stood.

"We've been here about thirty minutes or so. I didn't want to bother you; I know you're working," Naylor said, smiling, gently rubbing her thin frame against Craig.

"I can respect that. How are you, Brazil?" Craig said, now taking the seat to the right of Naylor.

"I'm good. How are you, Craig?" Brazil answered politely before taking a sip of her wine.

"I'm good as long as you're good," Craig said, chuckling before giving his attention back to Naylor. "I got a little something for you in the office. Give me about ten minutes and then meet me there. That all right with you?" Craig asked, as he slipped his hand under the table and rubbed her thigh.

That made her cringe on the inside. That meant he wanted to give her more than money in that office.

"Give me fifteen, I want to freshen up a little," Naylor said, whispering the last five words, careful to keep Brazil from hearing.

Craig sat there a few more minutes talking to Brazil more as to confuse anybody paying attention as to where his interest lay between the two women. When he got up, he stopped by a few more tables, doing the same thing he was at Naylor's table. She wondered how many other women he had besides her. She decided a long time ago that she didn't care, as long as he paid the bills she presented to him.

The band was on their tenth song and Brazil was on her fourth glass of wine. Naylor knew that was a bit much and was hoping she would be ready to go soon. She could tell Brazil was in her zone and was sitting on ready. Naylor was about to remind her of their conversation in the car, when she saw two familiar faces, one she already had on the hook and one she was working on.

"Good evening, ladies. These seats taken?" Naylor heard Jerome, one of the janitors from their school, along with Daelyn; the assistant superintendent of another school district.

"Even if they were, you two can take them," Brazil said, excitement in her voice.

"Naylor, is that cool with you?" Jerome asked, before sitting down.

"Of course. Why wouldn't it be?" Naylor asked, fake smile and all.

"Well, I am *just* the janitor," Jerome said, laughing out loud.

Brazil and Daelyn joined in the laughter.

Naylor didn't find what he said funny at all. She couldn't be upset at Brazil or Daelyn for laughing, as they would have no idea what the true connotation of the comment was.

Jerome was one of the guys she had a physical relationship with and money had nothing to do with it. From the moment she saw him with his work equipment, which consisted of a trash can, trash bags, mop, and broom, she was turned on. Her secret obsession for him had nothing to do with his work equipment but more so his looks. He was half Indian and half black and had the prettiest skin and hair she had seen on a janitor in her life. It only took her a couple of months to find herself in his janitor's closet, enjoying all of his equipment.

They had been a year into their secret closet adventures and Jerome was pushing for more. Naylor told him several times he was a fool if he thought she would go public with him knowing he was sleeping with some of the other teachers at the school.

"Besides, you're just a janitor. You can't afford to be my man," Naylor said to him during their last blow up.

Jerome's comment at the table solidified for her that no matter how many of her co-workers he was sleeping with, she was his number one closet crush. And in Naylor's mind, she was the winner.

"Ha, ha, very funny guys. If you would excuse me, I need to visit the ladies' room," Naylor said, cutting her eyes at Jerome when Brazil and Daelyn were out of eyeshot.

L. A. Logan

FIVE

It was close to 8:00 p.m. and Naylor had been ready to leave an hour ago. She had already collected $1500 from Craig and she didn't have to give him anything in return. She managed to dodge that bullet by telling him her monthly was paying her a visit. Craig had a thing about that, something to do with a woman's blood and a hex. He didn't even want to be in the same room as a woman he was involved with when she was going through her monthly homage, thanks to Eve and the serpent she allowed to haggle with her in the garden. The fact she knew Craig had a fear of what *might* happen if he knowingly made contact with a woman who was dealing with the monthly curse played in Naylor's favor.

Fifteen minutes later, Brazil was ready to go after Naylor noticed Daelyn had given her the head nod. Naylor was curious about a few things when it came to Daelyn. For the life of her she couldn't figure out how a man of his caliber was hanging out with the likes of Jerome; how on earth did dingy Brazil snag him and what it was going to take for her to get her claws in him?

Naylor was going to get as much information out of a tipsy Brazil as she could while on their drive back to the school. As the ladies headed toward the exit, Naylor discretely winked her eye at Jay, her way of letting him know he could still get it. Once she reached the door, two of Craig's trusty bouncers saw the two ladies to their car. She often wondered what Craig said to his workers as to why she had to be escorted to her vehicle. It really didn't matter to her, except for the few times a couple of them caught her eye. If she didn't fear Craig finding out, she would have test-driven one or two of them.

Brazil didn't have time to put her Civic in gear before Naylor wasted no time with the questions burning on the inside of her mind. The drive back to the school would take less than fifteen minutes and Naylor had to get at least two questions out the way. She decided to ask those first.

"Girl, how long have you and Daelyn been getting it in?" Naylor asked, pretending to be looking for something in her purse.

The usually guarded Brazil didn't hesitate to answer, and Naylor had the last three glasses of wine she had drunk to thank for that.

"Almost two years and counting," Brazil said, with a small smile on her face.

"Really, so you were dating him before he got his new job. That's cool. He seems like he is a good dude. I can't stand a man who has a good job and then treats you like he is doing you a favor by dating you," Naylor said, sounding irritated.

Brazil didn't miss a beat.

"Girl, I can't either. Daelyn is so not like that. He is a gentleman. He is running a tight race at winning my heart completely. I just need to get my life and stop playing games," Brazil said, laughing as if she had told a joke.

Naylor decided not to respond because she had a feeling Brazil was not done with her current thought and she was right.

"Like, I'm only twenty-four years old. What do I look like settling down with one man right now? I need at least another three or four years before I do that," Brazil said, as she exited the freeway.

"You mean to tell me you two aren't in a committed relationship?" Naylor barely got that question out of her mouth without sounding overjoyed.

"Girl, no. We are just hanging out, but if it were up to him we would be a *real* couple," Brazil said, as they waited for the stoplight to turn green.

Brazil had no idea what monster she had released with that last statement. She had just confirmed for Naylor that Daelyn and his wallet were open game and she was ready to take all the money out of it he would allow. By the looks of things, Brazil wasn't tapping into his wallet's full potential and before all was said and done, she would show Brazil what could have been, had she had her head in the game.

After basking in her small victory, Naylor had one more question she had to find out the answer to.

"Why is he hanging out with Jerome the janitor?" Naylor asked as they turned into the school parking lot.

"They have been best friends since high school," Brazil answered, right on cue.

"Really? Would have never guessed that. Does Jerome have a girlfriend?" Naylor asked, not really caring but always had to know who her would-be competition was.

"He is a fine one, ain't he?" Brazil said, some of the ghetto-ness she had kept bottled up all night was slowly starting to seep out.

"He's all right. Is he dating anyone?" Naylor rephrased her question.

Saying he was all right was an understatement. The janitor was an exact replica of former professional football player, Will Demps, standing 6'0" tall at 200 lbs. Pure muscle covered by unblemished caramel skin. He was beyond sexy to Naylor but still just a janitor, something her superficial mind would not allow her to get past. She knew looks couldn't pay the mounting bills she continually created for herself, but she still had to know who he was claiming as his woman.

"Yes, somebody at one of these schools, but Daelyn doesn't know who she is. Jerome keeps saying one day everybody would be shocked once they decided to go public," Brazil answered, pulling up next to Naylor's car.

"That sounds ridiculous. If they are in a relationship, why not go public? Have you met her? He probably has an imaginary girlfriend, Brazil," Naylor said, in a joking tone.

"Something about her job and them waiting until the right time. Nobody has met her but we know she exists." Brazil said, chuckling.

This caught Naylor's attention because nothing about her was funny.

"Why you say that?" Naylor asked, now looking directly at Brazil.

"Because *anytime* she calls, he drops *everything* for her. Got him whipped!" Brazil said, laughing even harder now.

That information fed Naylor's already larger-than-life ego and once again solidified that *she* was that girl and there was *nobody* who could knock her off her self-titled Diva throne. This was a far cry from the little insecure girl who used to sing in the youth choir and attend Vacation Bible School.

30

Before Naylor could push the start button on the car, her cell phone started ringing. It was none other than the janitor himself, which brought a conquering smile to her face. Naylor already knew what he wanted without him even having to ask and after hearing what Brazil had to say, she decided to muster up a little energy to oblige him as well as ensure her grip on his heart was tighter than it was the day before. Part of her knew she was wrong for playing games with this man but the other part, which was most dominant couldn't care less. He knew the game before he asked to be put in it and therefore he put himself at risk of getting hurt.

"Yes, you can stop by," Naylor said to Jerome before pulling out into traffic.

Naylor had collected all the money she needed to pay her bills for the month and She didn't even have to go to church and pray about it like so many of her co-workers would do. By all accounts, she seemed to be doing just fine making ends meet without crossing the church entrance every week. Now that all was well, she figured why not have a little fun without having to think about money and who better to do it with than the janitor.

L. A. Logan

Brazil

SIX

The traffic light couldn't change fast enough for Brazil as she sat at the intersection, blocks away from her apartment. She was beyond ready to get home and cuddle up with Daelyn for at least a few hours after he became the source that would help her release the stress and tension she had built up from the day's events. She wanted her night to end on a good note, unlike how her day started, and that would be her falling asleep next to his warm body.

As Brazil made her way down Runberg Lane, she did her best not to add another miserable dose of reality to her tipsy state of mind. From a distance she could see the luxury apartments she desperately wanted to make her home. They were a depressing reminder of how she once lived back when her life was good. If Brazil were sure she could pass the Breathalyzer test, she would break the speed limit in an effort to get the apartments quickly out of her sight and banish her wishful thinking.

Brazil Smith was born and raised in South Dallas in the Oak Cliff neighborhood. She was taught to be a lady by her parents, but her neighborhood surroundings infiltrated her soul and made her half lady, half hood. That was the only way she would survive the crime-infested area she called home.

Brazil was not ashamed of where she came from and had no problem letting you know not to let her sweet personality deceive you. She was one part bougie, one part ghetto, and proudly referred to herself as boughetto when necessary. Oftentimes people would tell her how nice and sweet she was. Brazil would let them know that's exactly how they wanted her to stay, nice and sweet, but when necessary she would give them a dose of her nice-nasty attitude. The nice-nasty would usually be enough for most to leave her alone. There would be the rare occasion when she would have to unleash her alter ego, Bri Bri, who was like a beautiful pit bull charging its target in slow motion while going in for the kill.

Brazil stood 5'7" tall, which was complimented by her toned 150lb. frame. She has always considered herself beautiful and any man's dream. She graduated from college at the top of her class and soon after accepted a well-paying job at a private school. It seemed she was living her dream; recently engaged to the love of her life, living in an affluent area of town, shopping on demand and taking dream vacations. It seemed life couldn't get better and all seemed so perfect until three years ago.

Brazil pulled into her parking space and felt humiliation wash over her. She knew it was the wine and her emotions that had been tag teaming against her all night. She hated living in The Gates apartment complex; especially knowing it was the downgrade to The Gates on The Hill, where Naylor lived.

That thought alone made her race into her apartment and pour another glass of wine. She hated drowning her emotions in bottle after bottle of wine, but it seemed to be the only thing that understood where she was coming from. As Brazil prepared to pour another glass of wine, she heard the soothing voice of the man who seemed to be the only one who got her and was willing to accept her for who she was.

"Baby, I think that is enough for tonight. Here, take this. It will help you feel better in the morning," Brazil heard Daelyn say, handing her a BC aspirin to take.

"I'm sorry, baby. Today was just crazy, you have no idea what happened," Brazil said, before pouring the white powder in her mouth and then following it with a few large swallows of Diet Coke.

"I'm sure it's not something we can't get past. Actually, for the rest of tonight, let's leave it in the past. Besides, I have news that will cheer you up," Daelyn said, gently kissing her on the hand.

"What?" Brazil asked as she felt a little life come back into her body.

Daelyn had a way of doing that to her.

"Well, I heard from a good source that they are looking at you for one of the assistant principal positions at your school," Daelyn said, smiling, knowing he'd just scored points with her.

Brazil couldn't believe what she was hearing. She already knew one of the positions was accounted for and just knew Naylor would be the second choice.

"What about Naylor?" Brazil asked, not sure if her hearing was clouded by the wine.

"What *about* Naylor? You care more about her than you do yourself?" Daelyn asked, bothered by her response.

"Well, she is one of my co-workers who has been at the school a lot longer than I have. Why would they give the job to me instead of her? Please tell me *you* didn't have anything to do with it," Brazil said with pleading eyes.

"First off, let me make two things clear. I had *nothing* to do with your name coming up as a strong contender. Your resume did that for you, Brazil. Second, Naylor's reputation precedes her and not in a good way. It probably would be a good idea to disassociate yourself from her. Trust me when I tell you this, *if* you do get selected over her, which I'm sure you will, you need to watch your back. If she has any information on you, she will use it to her advantage," Daelyn explained, concern in his tone.

Hearing those last words seemed to sober Brazil up a little. She had heard from many of the other teachers that nobody wanted to be on Naylor's bad side. She even remembered being told that several teachers had left or been transferred because they refused to deal with her.

Brazil couldn't recall any negative interactions she personally had with Naylor. Naylor always seemed to be so friendly and helpful to Brazil, never asking for anything in return. When she first arrived at the school, Naylor went out of her way to take her under her wing and showed her the ropes. It was hard for Brazil to imagine Naylor being the mean spirited and vindictive woman she had been hearing about the past two years.

"Honey, are you sure?" Brazil asked, not sure what to believe.

"Yes, I'm sure about the job and Naylor. Now if you don't mind, I'm done talking for the night and ready to be wrapped around my lady," Daelyn said, pulling her into him.

Brazil was excited at the idea of her career getting back on track. If she was to get the job, maybe she could reconcile with her ex-fiancé. The thought of leaving broke in her past and being able to get her old life back made the day's earlier events worth it.

SEVEN

It had been a month since Daelyn told her about the assistant principal job and Brazil had not heard anything. The water cooler talk said nobody else had heard anything either. Brazil refused to ask Daelyn anything else about the job, especially since he had not brought it back up anymore. When she woke up that morning, she willed the thought of even being considered for the job out of her mind. She figured this would help when she did receive the call that someone else was selected for the job.

Brazil couldn't help but wonder if Naylor had heard anything, especially since she and Whitney were best friends. If she was to believe the rumors, Whitney was the reason Naylor was still working at the school, which would have to mean Whitney wanted her for the job as well. If Brazil were to believe that, she would have to believe every other negative thing she had heard about Naylor too.

Brazil remained on the fence about this evil Naylor everyone had been telling her about. She figured by remaining on the fence, she could see things clearer and fairer this way.

"Good morning, lady! I brought your favorite this morning." Brazil looked up and saw Naylor standing in the doorway of her classroom, smiling ear to ear.

"Hey, girl. You didn't have to do that," Brazil said, looking at the bag in Naylor's left hand from Rachel's Bake Shop.

Naylor walked over to Brazil's desk and set the bag containing two large cinnamon rolls down. Brazil hadn't noticed the brown cardboard tray Naylor had containing two plastic cups of orange juice.

"Girl, yes I did. I have a huge favor to ask and knew I needed to butter you up a little beforehand," Naylor said, letting out a little laugh.

"Naylor, I told you I wasn't going out after work for a while. I was so hung over the last time we went out, I was too ashamed to even face my guy the next morning. I don't want to go through that again no time soon," Brazil said, laughing along with Naylor.

"Girl, what I have to ask you has nothing to do with a club or drinking, for that matter. It's work related," Naylor said, before taking a small bite of her cinnamon roll.

Naylor's request caught Brazil by total surprise. *What work-related favor could she possibly need me to do when Whitney is her best friend?* Brazil thought to herself. Maybe it was something Whitney couldn't ethically be affiliated with.

"What do you need me to do girl?" Brazil asked, taking a sip of her orange juice.

"Aren't you still affiliated with Daelyn?" Naylor asked, nonchalantly.

Brazil's Oak Cliff spider senses stood to attention. *What does Daelyn have to do with anything concerning Naylor?* Brazil thought to herself.

"We are cool. What's up? What does he have to do with anything?" Brazil asked, a hint of defensiveness in her tone.

"Girl, pipe down. I don't want your dude! Don't go ghetto on me so early in the morning, after all, I did bring you breakfast. I just need his help with something, that's all," Naylor said, in a serious tone.

Brazil could still sense something wasn't right, but she couldn't put her finger on it.

"Okay. What?" Brazil asked, no longer hiding her defensiveness.

"For you not to really like this dude, you sure are protective of him. Let me hurry up and tell you what I need before you jump on me," Naylor laughed slightly, as if she was playing.

Brazil's facial expression didn't change and she didn't say one word, but her body language was doing enough talking on its own.

"Anyway, you know I applied for the assistant principal job, right?" Naylor asked.

"Yes," Brazil said, no change in her face or tone.

"Well, I heard they are looking at someone else for the job and I have no idea who it is," Naylor said before Brazil cut her off.

"Naylor, he wouldn't know who the person is. He doesn't work for *our* board, remember?" Brazil said, frustration in her voice.

Brazil wasn't sure why she became frustrated. Was it because Naylor would have no scruples about asking her to do something so unethical and this might be a small glimpse into the self-centered Naylor she had heard about? Maybe it was because Brazil just might be the person Naylor was trying to find out about. Either way, Brazil knew she had to play her cards right while navigating through this conversation.

"I know that, girl. I want you, as my *friend*, to tell him to write a letter of recommendation for me and send it in to our board. That's all," Naylor said, smiling from ear to ear.

Brazil couldn't believe what Naylor had just asked. *That's all.* Brazil replayed Naylor's last two words in her mind.

Brazil was so shocked at Naylor's matter-of-fact tone that she was slow to speak, almost speechless. A million thoughts played over in her mind while observing Naylor's attitude and behavior that followed her request and it was like a curtain had been pulled back to reveal a large stage full of unfavorable props. If Brazil wasn't sure before, she was now; the real Naylor she had heard so much about was now sitting across from her sharing breakfast and it suddenly hit her that Daelyn's effort to help her peep game was valid.

EIGHT

"What makes you so sure he'll be willing to write the letter?" Brazil asked Naylor as they headed to the teachers lounge.

"Because you're sleeping with him, that's why. I thought that part would be a no brainer for you," Naylor said, annoyed.

The two didn't get to finish their earlier conversation because one of Brazil's students needed tutoring. Brazil told Naylor they would finish over lunch, though in reality she hoped Naylor would change her mind after rethinking the request.

"Let me get this straight. You want me to seduce Daelyn in an effort to convince him to recommend you for a promotion, which would make you one of my bosses?" Brazil asked, now stopping to look at Naylor.

"Yes, that's exactly what I'm saying," Naylor responded, looking at her as if it was no big deal.

"Let me ask you something, Naylor. Would you sleep with Craig in an effort to ask him to help me be your boss?" Brazil asked, looking Naylor in the eye.

"Girl, you're looking at this all wrong. I wouldn't just be your boss; I would be your safe haven. If one of us got this job, I mean if you had actually applied for the job, and one of us got it, we could have each other's back. You have to look at this as a win/win, girl," Naylor said, smiling as if she had won her case.

Once again Brazil was speechless at the fact that Naylor really believed the lie she had just told. She was unsure how you rationalized with a delusional person, especially on the job, but she had to come up with something fast. It became clear that Naylor wasn't going to let this go.

"I don't know how comfortable I would be using him like that," Brazil responded.

"I'm confused, Brazil. I thought you really didn't like dude like that," Naylor asked, becoming pushy.

"What gave you that idea?" Brazil asked, pushing back.

"The last time we went out, you told me you weren't feeling him like that. You said you were too young to give him what he wants," Naylor said, looking at her intently.

"I don't remember saying that. Maybe it was the alcohol," Brazil said, now ready to cut the conversation short.

"Is that so. I don't remember it being that way but okay, whatever. So, are you telling me you're not going to ask him?" Naylor asked, her tone cold as ice.

"No, that's not what I'm saying. Give me a couple of days and I will let you know what I find out," Brazil offered.

"That's all a girl can do. Now, if you feel more comfortable with me talking to him, I really don't have a problem with that," Naylor said, a hint of sexiness in her tone.

"That won't be necessary. I got this," Brazil said, a hint of sarcasm in her voice.

The two ladies exchanged a few more words that had nothing to do with the job. During the exchange Brazil's mind was working overtime. She was concentrating so hard on how she responded to Naylor that she felt her head was going to explode.

After hearing the next class bell ring, Brazil headed to the office to check her messages before heading back to her classroom. She saw Naylor walking and talking to Eddie, the Teacher's Aide. She had been trying to get information about him from Naylor but she wasn't saying much that Brazil didn't already know.

Brazil was doing her best not to be annoyed that out of all the schools in Austin, Eddie, her ex, would be teaching at her school. If she was being honest with herself, she was hurt that he made it clear that she was to say nothing to anybody about their past. His rationale for the secrecy was it was for the best, to give them both a fresh start. Brazil was confused about who was actually getting a fresh start out the deal, especially since she was still hopelessly in love with him.

L. A. Logan

NINE

As Brazil closed the door to her classroom she saw Eddie and Naylor sharing a laugh before they entered their classrooms. It was the same laugh she remembered sharing with Eddie not so long ago. The same laugh she would love to share with him again if only he would let her.

Once her door was closed, Brazil focused in on her class lesson for the next forty-five minutes. Constantly forcing out thoughts of her former fiancé being right across the hall just about took the place of the lesson. The only thing that kept her on task was her students and their constant questions in preparation for their test.

Once the last bell rang and her 9th grade students exited, Brazil closed the door to her room before returning to her desk. She decided not to take work home with her for once and started grading papers until the student she agreed to tutor showed up. Brazil wouldn't normally agree to an after school tutoring session but figured there was no reason to rush out to the ghetto she called home. The thought of going home only to sit there alone with a bottle of white wine and her pitiful feelings was depressing and not an option.

Fifteen minutes after class let out, Brazil's student showed up with her math book in hand. She worked with

Kylie for another hour before they had finished. Despite her mind being all over the place, Brazil was confident Kylie would pass her test with flying colors.

After seeing Kylie down the hall, Brazil once again caught a glimpse of Eddie coming out of Naylor's room, this time throwing the army-fatigue--colored backpack he was carrying over his shoulders. She stood there and secretly watched him as he made his way down the hall. *How on earth did we end up here?* Brazil asked herself, after Eddie was out of eyesight she headed back into her room to gather her things. She was emotionally drained and was not about to take it out on her students by way of her red marker, after all they didn't deserve to be on the receiving end of her frustrations.

The walk to her desk along with the thoughts flooding her mind, made each step harder and heavier to take in her Vince Camuto pumps. She no longer could control her emotions as the tears started to fall.

"Why do I keep doing this to myself?" Brazil said out loud.

"What exactly is it you keep doing, young lady?" Brazil heard Naylor say, turning to see her standing in the doorway.

"Girl, you scared the mess out of me! How long have you been standing there?" Brazil asked, the palm of her right hand resting on her chest.

"Long enough to know you got something on your mind. What's going on with you? You know you can talk to me about anything," Naylor said, taking a seat in front of Brazil's desk.

Brazil had to do a double take, as this was the exact same way her day had started, the only thing that was different was she wasn't sharing a meal with Naylor this time.

"No, seriously. I know I closed the door behind me. How did you creep that old decrepit door open without so much as a sound, without me knowing?" Brazil asked, purposely changing the subject.

Brazil wasn't going to tell Naylor what was on her mind, even if her life depended on it. It may have taken a little time, but she was starting to see a different side to Naylor, the side everyone else around her already knew.

"I wasn't standing there long. I guess you didn't hear me because your mind was somewhere else?" Naylor asked, now handing her a Kleenex, not letting up.

"Or, maybe I didn't hear you because you intentionally tried to sneak up on me," Brazil said, ignoring the Kleenex and with a hint of attitude in her voice.

Brazil's attitude had gone from sadness to madness in no time at all.

"Okay, I don't know what your problem is, but what you're not going to do is take out your anger on me. I'm just trying to be a friend to you, not like you have anybody else beating down your door checking on you," Naylor said, shaking her head.

Before Brazil could respond, her ringing cell phone interrupted the many unpleasant words she was going to unleash on Naylor. She didn't immediately recognize the number but decided to answer anyway.

"This is Brazil," she said, giving Naylor an ugly look.

Brazil wanted Naylor to know that their conversation was far from over.

"Girl, I don't have time for this. Stop by my room before you leave," Naylor demanded before leaving out the door.

Brazil quickly got up and walked over to the door to ensure she was really gone. She closed and locked the door behind her as she intently listened to the information the caller was giving her.

"So, if you're still interested and agree to the terms I briefly went over, we would like to offer you the Assistant Principal position," Brazil heard Debbie, one of the board members that was a part of the interview panel say.

"Of course, I would be honored," Brazil said, looking over at the door to ensure Naylor had not slipped back in without her knowledge.

After Debbie went over a few more details and set up a date and time to sign paperwork, Brazil hung up the phone and did a little dance. She was beyond happy and quickly over the depression that was trying to consume her fifteen minutes earlier.

Brazil's phone rang again, this time she did recognize the number.

"Hey, honey! I just got the call!" Brazil said, barely able to contain her joy.

"Congratulations, Ms. Brazil! Now, where would you like to go celebrate this evening?" Daelyn asked.

"I have a taste for P. F. Chang's," Brazil said, gathering her things.

She couldn't get the stacks of papers situated in their respective folders fast enough. After getting everything neatly put away, Brazil ended her phone call and focused on how she would get out the building without Naylor taking notice.

TEN

Brazil was floating through traffic as she hurriedly made her way home to get ready for her dinner date and celebration. She was reeling off the news that in two weeks she would be the assistant principal in charge of the 9th and 10th graders. She could hardly believe her life was slowly getting back on track. It had been a long three years but it was finally turning around and she was beyond glad about it. Living hand to mouth was not living as far as she was concerned.

Brazil remembered when it was Eddie she rushed home to and how wonderful he made her feel. His parents had truly raised him to be a gentleman and to know how to treat a woman. If he made it home before her, dinner would be cooked and her bubble bath would be waiting. As soon as she would hit the door, he insisted all she had to do was come in and put her feet up.

Brazil met Eddie during her sophomore year of college and it was love at first sight. At the time she was in a relationship with her high school sweetheart, David, but their relationship had already started to slowly unravel.

Brazil knew she and David were on two different paths, but she refused to break things off with him, mainly because

49

he was all she knew. When David was kicked out of school for selling marijuana, her parents begged her to end things with him. They believed he would become a distraction and she would lose focus on completing school. She refused, thinking everyone makes poor choices from time to time and he was no exception.

When David started having kids with random females and blaming it on Brazil because she wasn't there to take care of him, she felt conflicted. Against her better judgment, her parents and with baby number three on the way, she made plans to transfer schools just to be closer to him. By that time he wasn't working and wasn't going to school but he had promised if she came, he would get his act together for her.

The night before she was to move, Brazil prayed and asked God for a sign if she was making the right decision concerning her life. She even specifically asked that it be something so minor, but major at the same time.

The next morning while gathering her things, Brazil tried to call David to let him know she would be on her way. Her phone had frozen on one screen and was not responding to any of the touch commands she was trying. She was beyond aggravated since it was the fourth time in a month this had occurred.

Brazil headed straight to the cell phone store, without taking the battery out of her cell phone as a quick fix while aggravated her trip would be delayed. She was hoping to have her phone fixed in time to get on the road and still arrive at a decent time. She entered the familiar store and headed to the repair desk located in the back of the store. Once there she saw Eddie, a face she had not seen there before. He was a breath of fresh air.

Eddie was the color of dark chocolate and had the deepest dimples Brazil had ever seen on a man. His voice was smooth and full of confidence and his 6'4 frame appeared to be in perfect shape under his uniform. After taking in his amazing looks and the good smelling cologne he had on, Brazil momentarily forgot why she was there.

"Okay, Ms. Smith, give me about an hour and I should have your phone ready for you," Brazil remembered him saying.

She did as he said and returned to the store twenty minutes shy of an hour. She wasn't sure if it was her road trip or his good looks that had her come back early.

"We have you all fixed up. Hopefully you won't have the same problem, but if you do, please come back and we will replace the phone," Eddie said, smiling while handing her the phone back.

"Uh, what if I'm living out of town?" Brazil asked, mesmerized by his hazel eyes.

She remembered Eddie pausing for a moment before speaking.

"That would be a shame. I've seen you the last three times you came in and had been working up my courage to ask you out," Eddie said, showing her the dimples she would soon fall in love with.

Brazil decided not to leave town that weekend, at first blaming it on her phone and then eventually breaking things off with David for good. She and Eddie became inseparable. She finished school, and landed an unbelievable job while Eddie continued to work part-time and go to school.

They were engaged a year and a half later and living a life at the age of twenty-four that most twice their age could only dream of. It was perfect until that fateful day that changed everything.

Brazil pulled into one of the empty parking spaces in front of her apartment building and noticed that Daelyn hadn't arrived yet. She gathered her things and started walking towards her apartment door. As she unlocked the door her cell phone started ringing. Once inside she checked the caller id to see it was Naylor calling and decided not to answer.

"I can't do this with you right now!" Brazil said out loud before putting her phone on the charger in her small living room and heading to her bedroom.

Brazil had successfully bypassed all of Naylor's questions before leaving the school and had made it to her car without incriminating herself concerning the job. Right before she walked out the side door of the school, she heard Naylor's voice.

"Brazil! Brazil! I just got an email saying I wasn't selected for the job. Can you believe this? Something about them picking someone who was more qualified. Are you kidding me? Who could be more qualified than I, when I've been here longer than anyone, besides Whitney?" Naylor griped.

Brazil felt, under the circumstances, she should remain silent while Naylor continued with her rant.

"Girl, I just can't believe this! Mark my words, *whoever* this person is; I give you my word I'm going to make life here at William Hall their worst nightmare. They won't last six months if I have anything to do with it," Naylor said, clearly angry as she walked out the door, heading towards her car.

Brazil remembered saying nothing as she watched Naylor get into her vehicle, fussing the entire time before screeching out of the parking lot. Brazil could do nothing but shake her head at the sight of her bitter and self-centered co-worker. The one thing she was grateful about was the two-headed snake had just revealed herself before slithering away.

L. A. Logan

Layla

54

ELEVEN

The vibrating noise echoing off Layla's marble end table took her attention from the book she was hopelessly lost in. She was growing frustrated by the minute because this was the fourth time in the last thirty minutes her phone demanded her attention. If it had not been for the three phone calls she was expecting, she would set her phone to silent mode and be done with it.

Layla, an avid book reader, had started on a new book, Last Temptation, she'd picked up at Sam's while waiting for the new tires she had purchased to be placed on her car. The book had just started to get good when Patricia made the crazy decision to give her ex another chance, even though he was living with another woman at the time. Funny thing, Layla knew a few women like that, especially the one that was calling her phone at that moment.

"Hey, lady! What are you up to?" Layla said, answering her phone, as she book- marked her place before putting the book down.

"Nothing much. What are you up to?" Coco asked, sounding a little down.

"You know me, settling into my Friday evening after a long week," Layla said, taking a sip of her ice cold Hawaiian Punch.

"Let me guess, Darrel is out of town on business, you have your pajamas on while turning the electronic pages of love on your Nook. What's your drink of choice tonight? Hawaiian Punch or Apple Juice?" Coco asked, in a teasing tone.

Layla could do nothing but laugh at Coco's statement, mainly because she was right and there was little she could say to discount her friend's synopsis of her life.

Coco knew better than anyone the lifestyle Layla had comfortably settled into. At the ripe old age of twenty-seven, she was living like one of the church mothers that she attended weekly noon day prayer with.

"You're laughing because you know what I'm saying is true. Admit it already Layla," Coco said, laughing along with Layla.

"Okay, fine! Yes, my man is out of town on business, I've got on a pair of my new pajamas, and drinking a glass of Hawaiian Punch. The one thing you are wrong about is *how* I'm reading. I'm actually holding a book in my hand, thank you very much!" Layla responded, glad she could prove at least one of her friend's statements wrong.

"We need to do something about this. You're too young to live like you're eighty years old, honey. You need some excitement in your life," Coco said, this time with a little less laughter.

Layla Massey was pretty content with her life, although there were times she had a bout or two with loneliness. She was 5'2" and was considered thick around the bases but in all the right places. Her weight was something she had struggled with since her early twenties; currently her weight was 192lbs, and she was okay with it.

The fact that Darrel fully embraced her curves and her judgmental attitude, made her even more comfortable in her skin. Layla was happy with her life. She was working a job she enjoyed, minus the drama and had finally found a church she was happy in. If there was one thing missing, it was the ring and the kids, but she could honestly wait another two years before that became a major priority on her list of things left to accomplish.

As Layla listened to all of Coco's ideas of what she needed to do in order to spice up her boring life, she could do nothing but laugh on the inside. In Layla's mind, how could a chick whose love life regularly played out like a Lifetime movie give advice to her. She had shared her opinion with Coco on many occasions concerning the subject of love.

"Coco, I think I got this. After all, I am doing much better in the love department than you are, if I must say so myself," Layla said, interrupting Coco's last sentence.

"I didn't say you didn't have it Layla, I was just trying to give you a little friendly advice, that's all," Coco said, tone defensive.

"And I appreciate it. Now, I'm sure that's not why you were calling. Surely you weren't calling to spice up my love life," Layla said, clearly done with the subject as it pertained to her.

"Well, actually, I wanted to see if you were available to do lunch and a movie tomorrow," Coco asked, ignoring Layla's flipped attitude in order to keep the tone light.

"Yes, I would love to. What movie do you want to see?" Layla asked.

"Think Like a Man Too," Coco said, with a hint of sarcasm in her voice.

"So they dropped Act Like a Lady from the title or did you?" Layla said, with a slight laugh.

"I can't do this with you right now, Layla, besides, Qarius just got here. I will see you tomorrow at our favorite place at noon. Love you, sis, bye," Coco said, not allowing Layla to respond.

The laugh Layla had stifled had now been given permission to escape the silence that held it captive in order to spare Coco's feelings. She picked her book back up and began reading again. Hoping she could get through the next chapter without the phone ringing again. She did manage to make that happen right before she heard the buzzing noise coming from the table her phone was resting on.

She looked over and was glad to put her book down for the incoming call from Darrel. His was one of the three calls she was expecting.

TWELVE

Layla had been dating Darrel for almost two years and as far as she was concerned, things were outstanding between the two of them. He seemed to show up in her life right when she felt the world was quietly falling apart around her.

At that time, she was fresh off a very emotionally abusive relationship and all self-esteem had been sucked out of her. On top of finding herself single, the trust fund that had been set up by her paternal grandparents was gone. Her ex had literally drained her bank account down to the minimum amounts that were required to still be considered a customer.

When she started to receive late notices on all of her many credit cards she didn't panic. She figured she would only keep up with the ones that really mattered. That worked for a while until she started getting shut-off notices from the local utility companies and when the eviction notice came from the office that managed the condos she lived in, that's when reality sank in.

When she went to her parents for help, she was hit with yet another unexpected blow. Layla's parents refused to help her out of the mess she had found herself in and told her she needed to get rid of the dead weight and needed to get a grip on life.

"What did you do with all that money? Are you on drugs or have just lost your mind completely?" Layla remembered her father asking.

She remembered his eyes being bright red like fire and his breathing was heavy. With each word he spoke, he seemed to grow angrier by the second. She knew deep down inside he wasn't angry with her for spending the money, but more so for getting caught up with Kelvin to begin with.

"Your father and I have worked very hard to send you to the very best schools so you could get a great education. Your grandparents left you that money so you could comfortably settle into your career and start a family with a *husband*! We didn't do all that for you to squander every penny you had in the bank with some undeserving tick of a man that the only thing he has to offer is what's swinging between his legs!" Layla remembered her mother fussing.

"I mean, Layla, for goodness sake, if that's all you required from a man, you could have gotten that from just about any one of them and I'm sure it wouldn't have cost you over one hundred and eighty thousand dollars either!" That was the last thing Layla's mother said before she walked out of the family room on that day.

Layla never forgot the look of disappointment on both her parents' faces that Sunday afternoon. The last thing she wanted to do was disappoint the people she knew loved and cared about her. She took what they said to heart and managed to get her life back on track.

The first thing Layla did on her list was set a plan in motion to end her toxic relationship with Kelvin. That was one of the hardest things for her to do, mainly because her heart was still in it. Although he had cost her so much;

ironically, she wasn't focused on the money, but was more so devastated about having to break up with him. She was hurt mainly about him no longer being a part of her life along with the time and feelings she could never get back.

Kelvin Matterson was a bad boy; her bad boy and she loved him with every fiber of her being. In her eyes he could do no wrong and if he did, nobody else could speak on it. Even after the demise of their relationship, it took a few years to truly move the love she had for him into the vault that was located in the back of her heart. There were so many things she did for him that no other living soul knew anything about. So many things they went through as a couple that most would never experience in a lifetime. Things that kept her going back for more, even when she knew the outcome would never be different. When she finally convinced him that it was over and had no contact with him, she felt like she was dying a slow death. Each day she would go without hearing from him, she just knew that would be the day she would die an unhappy woman. No matter how unequipped Kelvin was at being a man, he had a wonderful heart and he was the love of her life.

Of course Layla didn't see any of this the day they met at Enterprise Rent-A-Car. She had been in an accident the day before and was there to pick up a rental. She was in somewhat of a bad mood because she was not looking forward to car shopping with her dad. Mainly because she knew he wouldn't let her get what she wanted, regardless of the fact she had $250,000 dollars sitting in the bank with her name on it.

Kelvin was standing behind the counter assisting another customer but couldn't keep his eyes off her. Layla couldn't keep her eyes off his caramel colored skin and his brown eyes. It was like a spark quietly went off between the two of them, all before they even exchanged one word.

Once Layla reached his counter for assistance, the rest was history. She was happy she had convinced her father to wait in the car. The two began dating and did so the next four years until Kelvin's constant unemployment, marijuana smoking, alcohol consumption, and partying got the best of her and her bank accounts.

After dealing with all of that, Darrel was a welcome breath of fresh air. He seemed to help ground her in many ways and the areas in which he had not accomplished that, they'd learned to compromise. He would always tell her as long as she was happy, he was happy.

Layla did have one thing she still struggled with and that was how easy it was for her to have a strong opinion on what everyone had wrong in their lives without reflecting on where her life used to be. The one thing that was a plus, Layla knew she had this issue and needed to do better. The other, was Darrel loved her in spite of herself, and for that she was grateful.

She decided to give the man on the other end of the phone her full attention instead of letting fleeting thoughts of her past take up any additional space in her already overworked mind.

THIRTEEN

"Hey, you," Layla said, closing her book along with thoughts of Kelvin.

"How's my lady doing this evening?" Darrel asked.

"I'm *doing* my usual," Layla said, emphasizing the second word.

"Baby, why didn't you hang out with some of your friends tonight instead of holding your couch hostage?" Darrel asked, with a chuckle.

Layla knew that question was coming. She had asked herself that same question many times, but she had a great excuse for staying in this evening.

"I'm keeping the baby for Rhae and Kurt. It's their anniversary and first night out since she gave birth three months ago," Layla responded.

Kurt was her older brother and Rhae was his wife of five years. Their love story was a lifetime movie, but more on the positive side. They met at the bar scene, had sex the same night and had been inseparable ever since. Layla hadn't given their relationship five months but here they were, seven years and a baby later, still happy and in love.

At first Layla thought Rhae was only hanging around because of her brother's trust fund but was made to put that theory to rest when she found out otherwise. When she discovered her brother had never told Rhae anything about his true financial situation until after they were married, she was left speechless.

That revelation made Layla feel like an idiot for accusing her now sister-in-law of doing the same thing to her brother that she was allowing her then man—who was nowhere close to even being a fiancé, let alone a husband—to do to her. She had nobody to blame but herself for telling Kelvin all her financial business to begin with; especially knowing he was not the marrying type.

"How is Mia doing? Is she still a good baby?" Darrel asked.

"Of course, she is and as cute as she wants to be, just like her auntie!" Layla said, chuckling.

Keeping Mia filled the void in Layla's life of being childless and it also gave her the excuse she needed not to hang out with the few friends she had.

"Yes, she is and one day you will have a daughter and your brother will return the babysitting favor," Darrel offered, chuckling along with her.

Layla listened intently as Darrel talked about everything from her niece to his workday. She loved the sound of his voice as he talked with a tone of authority. He also knew how to reciprocate by listening to her talk about her day subbing at a school full of adults who acted more like the kids she was hired to teach.

Layla had been working at the school for the past three weeks and actually liked it most days. But there were those days when dealing with the likes of Naylor Jones, who thought she was flawless and thought she could talk to people like they had a tail between their legs, who gave her second thoughts. Yes, those days made Layla want to put down all the etiquette her parents had paid top money for, just to let Naylor know she didn't want what Layla Massey could bring to the yard.

Layla was born and raised in Austin with a close-knit family that was full of love. Unlike most of her friends, both parents were in the home and they spent a lot of quality time together. Her parents truly cared about her and her brother and did everything in their power to raise well-rounded productive children. The two of them grew up best friends and continued to be so. He never told their parents how he met Rhae and only trusted that information with Layla. She had also shared many things with Kurt that her parents had no clue about. They had grown up to be great adults by most people's standards and were closer than ever. Their bond was unbreakable, even after he figured out the type of man Kelvin really was.

"Sis, I don't think he's good for you. You can do much better than Kelvin," Layla remembered her brother saying on the day he discovered Kelvin was far from a one-woman man.

"He is just not used to being in a committed relationship and besides, we all make mistakes. I know what I'm doing brother so don't worry," Layla responded, which seemed to satisfy her brother at the time.

Kurt and Kelvin eventually became friendly, thanks to Layla's persistence in making Kurt help Kelvin feel like family. Kurt was reluctant at first but due to the love he had for his sister, he befriended Kelvin against his better judgment. She had convinced him this might help their parents accept Kelvin and take some of the pressure off of her. After being around Kelvin a short amount of time, Kurt immediately started seeing serious red flags.

"Does Kelvin still work at Enterprise Rentals?" Kurt asked one day while they were out shopping for a birthday gift for their mother.

"Of course he does. That is the fourth time in two months you've asked me that. Why is that?" Layla responded.

"Just asking," Kurt would say, perplexed look on his face while quickly changing the subject.

It wasn't long before Kurt told her Kelvin no longer worked there and refused to tell her how he knew at first. He didn't want to be in the middle of any potential problems the two were having but felt, as her brother, he had to tell her what he knew. After much pressure from her, he later explained to her that his job was in the middle of contract negotiations with Enterprise. When he asked the district manager about Kelvin, he advised he was no longer working for the company.

Kelvin not only had Layla under the impression he was working there but had her also thinking he was in management training. After her brother told her Kelvin had not been working there for at least the past two months, she was beyond hurt and confused. She wondered what made him think he had to lie to her about something so simple.

When Layla confronted Kelvin about the recent change in his employment status, he told her he thought he had told her about it. He did a great job of explaining it to her mind and also her body. When he got done taking them both for a ride, she didn't make a huge deal out of it, especially since he had a new management position with Avis Car Rental. As far as she was concerned it was an even wash and nothing to fuss over.

"What do you mean nothing to fuss over, sis? The man is a pathological liar and he means you no good. I'm a man's

66

man and we don't treat women we consider wife material this way. Get rid of him before he ends up hurting you, which will force me to get involved," Layla remembered that conversation all too well.

At the time, she was afraid that disagreement would cause a rift between her and her brother. After much prayer and conversation they were able to move past it while managing to keep both relationships intact. Kurt continued to keep his eye on Kelvin and Kelvin continued to fall down on his abilities to be a responsible man.

The job-hopping went on just about every three to six months along with the mind and body games he played with her. Slowly Kelvin wasn't able to pay his portion of the household bills or any of his personal bills. Layla would reassure him that she had it covered and not to worry about it. She insisted on taking care of them while he concentrated on making his next career choice.

Soon after his car was *stolen*, he had to use her vehicle to get back and forth to work. That didn't bother Layla so much until the aroma of freshly burned marijuana greeted her the moment she opened her car door. She was furious at the level of disrespect toward her car, especially since she wasn't a smoker of any kind. No matter how upset she was, fighting with him wasn't an option. Instead Layla did what she always did, she fixed the problem on her own so that Kelvin could focus on getting himself back on track. Layla was sure if her parents knew she purchased him a vehicle that year and signed the title over to him without him paying her one penny, they would disown her or worse, cut her out of their will.

The more she laid on her couch talking to her new love, she didn't regret the car or any part of her dysfunctional relationship with Kelvin; what she regretted the most was not ending the relationship sooner. Layla couldn't help but think had she done so, she would have a much softer heart and a mind that veered towards encouragement instead of judgment.

FOURTEEN

Layla heard baby Mia stirring, thanks to the baby monitor she had sitting on the end table. She wasn't surprised that her niece was up and demanding some attention from her auntie. She had slept four hours since her last feeding and diaper change and apparently was ready for round two.

Layla ended her phone conversation with Darrel and headed to the kitchen. She placed the plastic Playtex disposable liner inside the clear bottle that had been sitting on her black granite counter top. After filling it with milk she tightly turned the pink lid before placing it inside a warm glass of water. By the time she finished changing Mia's diaper and bringing her into the living room, the bottle was just right and ready for her feeding.

Layla admired her niece as she sucked on the six-ounce bottle filled with Enfamil formula. She had to admit that her brother produced a beautiful baby whom she loved to pieces. With the way Layla felt about Mia, she could only imagine how much love she would have for her own child one day. The thought brought tears to her eyes, and she didn't try to hide them this time. They were for kids she'd never allowed to have a chance at life, kids whose father she'd let convince her they weren't ready for.

"I told you I wasn't ready to have any kids! Why didn't you take care of yourself so this wouldn't happen?" Layla remembered Kelvin saying, clearly angry.

"I don't know, I just didn't. I thought we were moving in that direction with our relationship. I thought this might help us get settled down. I'm pregnant with twins this time, Kelvin," Layla said, in between tears.

She was trying not to become distraught during the conversation, especially after her parents made it painfully clear they would *never* accept Kelvin as a part of the family. In low esteem thought pattern, she was hoping a baby would bring everybody together.

"What do you mean, you don't know? I will tell you what I know, I need you to take care of this. Do you hear me? I'm not ready for another kid!" Kelvin said, picking up his keys and walking out the house.

That's how most of their discussions would end and there was nothing she could do about it. She should have known better, especially since this wasn't the first time he didn't have a problem letting her know how he felt about her being pregnant with his seed. The fact that he had two children with two other women while they were together but he continued to refuse hers was final confirmation of what her parents had been demanding her to do for months.

Layla took eight hundred dollars of the thousand she had in the bank and went to have her babies permanently removed. This time would be the last time she would find herself in this situation. That very next day she hired a moving company and had his belongings moved to his momma's house, changed her locks and security codes, sent him a break up text message and set out to start life without him. She blocked every number he could possibly call her from to keep herself from battling with the 'to answer or not to answer' game each time he might call. She completely blocked him out of her life while she mourned the loss of him as though he was dead.

Back then, Layla thought a baby would solve her problems, but seeing how Mia was born into the arms of two loving parents who were already on a solid foundation *before* she came into the world, gave Layla peace. She knew aborting her babies was not right, but she knew God had forgiven her and her three babies would never have to grow up in a destructive home life full of confusion and dysfunction.

After Mia finished her bottle, Layla used the burp cloth to wipe around her lips and neck to catch any milk that may have been missed. Layla then began to gently pat her on the back, adjusting the pink and yellow jumper she had on. Mia let out a few burps and Layla told Mia how much of a big girl she was. As she quietly sang a few songs to Mia, Layla's cell phone vibrated. When she looked over, it was Kurt who had sent a text saying they were on their way. She sent her brother a response and went back to spoiling her niece.

Once Mia fell back to sleep, Layla laid her on the pink and white blanket she had spread out on her chocolate brown couch. After making sure Mia was secure, she began to pack her bag just in case her brother was in a hurry. She told him Mia could stay all night so that he and his wife could have a night of wild fun, but they both declined. She didn't take it personally, figuring they weren't ready to let Mia stay the night away from home just yet. This was solidified for her since she was given the first opportunity to keep her and both sets of grandparents were available.

Layla's brother always made her feel special and always looked out for her. She had to admit that God must have broken the mold when he created Kurt. He lived a well-rounded life and was truly a good guy.

Kurt was the head City Engineer and was partly responsible for introducing her to Darrel. The city was always having some type of party for their employees and Kurt had finally convinced her to attend one with him. He had worked on her for months, constantly reminding her that Kelvin had clearly moved on and it was high time she did the same.

"While you are laying around here acting like your dad didn't show you love and your mom didn't show you what a hair comb and grease look like, Kelvin has moved on with his life," Layla remembered Kurt saying to her.

"My sister will not become a pole dancer all because one fool didn't realize her worth. Get up, Layla Jane, before I call your momma," Kurt said, laughing.

"Whatever! I wish you would call Mom over here. It would be so ugly the way I'm feeling right about now," Layla said, smoothing the covers over her limp body.

"Let me ask you something. Do you really think Kelvin is messed up over the break up? You know what . . . Don't answer that. I won't even set you up like that. He has moved on, sis and it's time you did the same," Kurt said, opening the bag of food from Wendy's he had set on the table.

Layla remembered that information stung her just a little. As she watched her brother unpack the food and set it up on her coffee table, she wondered how her brother knew what Kelvin was doing.

"Oh, really? And how do you know that?" Layla recalled asking after taking a bite of her French fry.

"I saw him today and we had a chance to catch up," Kurt said, taking a bite from his Wendy's cheeseburger.

Layla remembered it like it was yesterday. Kurt had brought her lunch for the third time that week while she was recovering from a bout of heartbreak.

"Where?" she asked.

"You know he is a supervisor with the city now. He is over the sanitation department," Kurt said, taking another bite.

"Supervisor?" Layla remembered saying out loud.

"Yes, supervisor. You forget how many jobs the man has had in his life. He qualified to be a shift supervisor in sanitation," Kurt said, jokingly.

Layla had decided not to ask any more questions for the sake of her stomach, but her brother didn't pick that up from her silence and continued his Kelvin update.

"He told me he was hurt after you dumped him but life moves on. He is dating this chick named Sheba Moody that works in the Parks and Recreations Department," Kelvin said, taking another bite from his sandwich.

"Oh, does he seem serious about her?" Layla remembered asking.

"Of course he does. He *seemed* serious when he was with you, but what did that mean? Look, sis, I'm not trying to hurt your feelings or anything, but you're much better off without him. It's been six months since you dumped dude, it's time to move on. He was not on your level and I'm surprised it took as long as it did to get tired of him," Kurt said, giving her another dose of tough love.

"I know, I know, but I just hate starting over. It's a pain in the butt to learn someone knew. I don't have the energy for all of that anymore," Layla remembered saying, fighting back tears concerning the reality of her life.

L. A. Logan

FIFTEEN

Layla did her best not to be envious of her beautiful sister-in-law who looked flawless as she hugged and kissed on her baby girl. She casually watched Rhae as she cooed over Mia, who seemed to instantly respond to the sound of her momma's voice. It was priceless.

Rhae looked like a woman who was truly happy and in love. She looked stunning even though she was just fifteen pounds shy of pre-baby weight and seemed to be wearing the lagging pounds very well. She had on an orange and white strapless Ralph Lauren dress complimented by a pair of black Jessica Simpson pumps accented with black and orange jewelry, all with coordinating make-up. Simply put, she looked perfect.

Layla did her best to keep up with every word coming out her brother's mouth while fixating on his wife. She made one night stands look like the best thing going. A jump off had nothing on Mrs. Kurt Massey, baby weight, and all.

"So, when will my dude be back in town? I want to hang out, get a little guy time in," Layla heard Kurt ask.

"Sometime tomorrow evening. I'm not positive of the time," Layla answered, giving her gawking eyes a break from Rhae and now packing the last of Mia's things into her Coach Baby Bag.

"Layla, why don't you two come over after church Sunday? We can throw something on the grill. It's been awhile since we've all hung out," Rhae asked, smiling ear to ear while gently situating Mia in her arms.

Layla had a love/hate obsession toward her sister-in-law and she knew it was past ridiculous after all these years. There was no doubt in Layla's mind that Rhae genuinely loved her and had no clue the secret ill will Layla had toward her, past and present.

Layla was glad Rhae was clueless about her unflattering thoughts, mainly because she knew they would make her look even more foolish than she felt. Now, if Layla could only reciprocate the same feelings Rhae had for her without letting her petty thoughts of jealousy get in the way that would be a huge battle won.

Sometimes Layla wondered if she could ever really tell someone how she felt when it came to Rhae without it causing a major dilemma within the dynamics of their family. If she could tell the whole truth and nothing but the truth so help her God in an effort to expose that very thing that at times held her captive, that would be a wonderful thing.

Rhae was living the life Layla so desperately wanted and she served as a constant reminder that she was nowhere near achieving it. Layla wanted the house, white picket fence, and everything that came with it, but it had to be a man that could capture the whole essence of her. Only one man, who was truly undeserving, had captured Layla's mind, body, and soul and the destruction he left behind was worse than an F5 tornado.

Layla knew she could have it again, but this time with Darrel, a man that truly deserved a woman like her. He treated her like she was the only woman in the world for him and that was something new for her. Everything would be good if she could only stop focusing on the one thing Darrel didn't have. She had actually convinced herself how unhappy she would be without this one thing. If not for that, she would be a happily married woman by now and would have something in common with the beauty sitting before her that was her sister-in-law.

"Sure, that sounds good, sister-in-law. I will make sure Darrel is available, I will confirm with you by tomorrow night," Layla said, handing Rhae the diaper bag.

Layla gave her niece another kiss good-bye before doing the same to her brother and his wife. After seeing her family out the door, Layla went back to the couch and picked up her vibrating phone that was lying next to the book that had served as her entertainment for the night. She had a text from Darrel who was telling her how much he missed her and couldn't wait to see her bright smile the following night. The message instantly made her feel warm all over, inside and out. As she responded back to the message, a smile came over her face as she thought back to the night they met. The more she thought about it, she owed her brother a thank you card for being the avenue to her current happiness.

Ironically it was the same day Kurt had floored her with the news of Kelvin's newfound job and love life. That was the day she was convinced you could be blessed and cursed all in the same day.

"Look, I need you to get up off this couch, get in some hot soapy water, do something with this nap ball of hair on the top of your head and put on the cutest little black dress you have! And don't try to play me like you don't have anything to put on. You got your trust fund payment and you can't tell me you haven't spent any of it," Kurt said, gently hitting the week old bun that was resting on the top of Layla's head.

"And why would I do that?" Layla asked, playfully moving his hand away from her head.

"Because you're hanging out with your big brother tonight and I'm not taking no for an answer. Rhae has to work late and I still have to go; it's a work function. Since I'm the boss I kind of have to be there. You will be my plus one this evening. I will be here to pick you up at 7:00 p.m. sharp," Layla recalled him saying.

Hating that her big brother was right about her money, she did as he instructed her to do. She figured a celebration was in order since God blessed her to get rid of the dead weight before he found out about the other money that was left for her. That made the urgency in her parents' request understandable. There was no way they could have sat back and watched her waste more money on nonsense.

Layla managed to even make it to the beauty shop, get dressed, and had fifteen minutes to spare before Kurt showed up at her doorstep. Once in the car, Kurt made small talk about work, Rhae, and how he was finally ready to start a family. Layla listened, feeling like a basket overflowing with nerves. As they pulled into the parking deck of the Hilton Hotel that was connected to the Austin Convention Center, she felt her heart skip a beat. For a brief moment she remembered her many lunch dates with Kelvin at the Hilton. She wondered if he had been treating his new girlfriend to lunch at the same place. Lucky for her, those thoughts were quickly interrupted.

"You look great, little sis," Layla remembered her brother saying right before he opened the door to the ballroom.

That gave her a little boost of confidence, which she was sure he knew she needed at that moment. After Kurt greeted a few people, they headed to the bar located along the center of the back wall. Once there, she ordered a Sprite and grenadine with two cherries. Layla wasn't a drinker but she knew how to mix and mingle without making those who did drink feel uncomfortable.

After two hours of dancing and mingling with her brother, she noticed a very confident medium height gentleman that was the color of chocolate milk walk through the door and everything about him commanded everybody's attention.

Layla could tell from a distance that he smelled as amazing as he looked and the infamous Ralph Lauren Horse resting on the right side of his button down shirt was fresh off the pressing board. She was positive his entire outfit of choice, including the shoes, were of high quality as well. Everything about him spoke class, something Layla hadn't had in a man in a very long time.

Looking at him, Layla just knew that arrogance was in a strong first place as part of his personality. As far as she was concerned, if it was, he had a right to be, as handsome as he was.

Layla casually watched him throughout the night, careful to see how many females flocked to him and how he handled each one. He had plenty of birds—mostly from the pigeon and chicken family—in his face but to her surprise he dismissed all of them back to the coup they came from. She was willing to bet her new found trust fund that he didn't have anything intimate going on with any of them. After dealing with Kelvin, she learned that body language told it all.

Layla's curiosity got the best of her after she saw Kurt engaging with him for several minutes. It was clear they were more than just causal coworkers and she made a mental note to ask her brother about him. Thirty minutes later her curiosity quickly turned to panic when she saw Kurt walking toward her with the man sent from heaven above in tow.

"Darrel, this is my sister, Layla; Layla, this is the man who runs all of Austin, Darrel," Kurt said, with a chuckle.

"All of Austin, you say?" Was all Layla could get out.

She was not expecting the gorgeous man standing in front of her to be in charge of the city she was born and raised in.

"Yes, all of Austin, he is *our* city manager," Kurt added.

After a few moments, Layla remembered reading something on the Internet about the new city manager but she never bothered to look at his picture. What she did remember was his resume looked great on paper and from what she saw before her, the man was more impressive than his resume.

"Your brother is always giving me a hard time. It's my pleasure to meet you, Layla," Darrel said, gently shaking her hand.

Layla remembered sizing him up and comparing him to Kelvin in that short amount of time. She almost didn't feel worthy of being in his presence after what she had been through with Kelvin.

The two of them talked nonstop for the next couple of hours and exchanged numbers at the end of the night. They talked on the phone for six months straight before she agreed to go out with him. After their first date, she knew he was marriage material, which was a plus. After the debacle with

Kelvin, she vowed only to date marriage material going forward.

When you lined him up next to Kelvin, there was no comparison. Darrel was the clear winner in the *real* man department. Layla often wondered what Darrel saw in her, but more importantly, what was the cause of her dragging her feet when it came to a true commitment to Darrel.

He had an outstanding job as the City Manager of Austin, wasn't bad on the eyes, and could carry on a conversation with anybody, regardless of their status in the working world. Darrel was truly comfortable in any setting he found himself in and made sure that whomever was in his company was just as comfortable.

He always went out of his way to make her feel comfortable. He never made Layla feel less than because she was a substitute teacher. She loved him unconditionally for that reason alone.

Layla responded back to Darrel's text and decided to call it a night. She had to have her mind right for her lunch date with Coco and her body rested for Darrel.

L. A. Logan

Whitney

SIXTEEN

With a chilled bottle of Red Electra California Moscato sitting on her end table, Whitney surveyed the small living room before taking another sip from the glass of wine. This was her second glass of the red wine that night and she was looking forward to at least one more before she called it quits. It had been one of the hardest weeks of work she could remember having since her promotion and she was desperately trying to relax. She just wanted to get rid of the stress that had invaded her body virtually without her knowledge until that afternoon. Before getting promoted, one glass of wine would usually do the trick, but as of this week she found herself drinking at least half a bottle a day in order to settle down.

Whitney was very excited about her new position as principal and knew it would be challenging but had no idea how difficult some would make her new role as the head lady in charge. It wasn't like she walked around with a hat on, advertising her new role within the school. As far as she was concerned, she was still the same Whitney she was prior to the extra zero's being added to her paycheck.

Whitney had tried new things in an effort to help acclimate her staff into her new role in their lives. She did

83

her best to ignore some of the sly comments she heard about how she got the job to begin with.

"You know she dated the brother of the uncle who serves on the board" or "She only got the position because she is black," that one had to be the most hurtful. People insinuating you got a job because you either knew somebody or had slept with somebody at the top was an old cliché' that had been around for years. The one that bothered Whitney the most had to do with skin color. She hated when anyone, including her own people, would throw the race card out like it was the Big Joker in a Spades card game.

Whitney had worked very hard for her promotion and was willing to put in the work to show she was beyond worthy to have the job. At times she wanted to get on the office PA system and announce all of her degrees, experience, and how many people she didn't know who worked on the hiring board for the school. She always ended up deciding against it because at the end of the day, folks will believe what they want to believe, no matter who had said or seen it.

She was doing her best not to have second thoughts about accepting the offer to stay at the high school to rule over those who were her peers the year before instead of moving over to the Junior High. She felt like moving would give the impression she couldn't handle the pressure and she wasn't going to give anyone the satisfaction of talking about that each time she walked by and thought she was out of earshot. As she took another gulp of her wine, she was beginning to think maybe they were right, and she should have gone to a school where they didn't know her so well.

Prior to partaking in her choice of drink, she had been in her master bathroom crying her eyes out. At first, Whitney couldn't figure out why she had allowed work to get her so emotional. There was no way she could continue to drown her emotions and thoughts in bottle after bottle of wine each evening when she got home. She had to wrap her mind around the source of her contention and she needed to do that quickly. After all, she was the boss and at the end of the day, what she said was law and it didn't matter who she was dealing with.

After crying for what seemed like hours, Whitney knew she had to shake the negative energy off and get her mind back in the game. There was no time for her mind to take her down the road of depression. She had way too much on her plate to be feeding into an emotion that had caused her so much pain in the past.

Whitney Maxton was the average girl next door with a big heart and willingness to help anybody. A trait that was responsible for her heart being mishandled many times during her lifetime. Despite how life around her changed without warning, Whitney always tried to maintain the love for others that was instilled in her.

Born and raised in Austin by her father's sister Roberta, whom she called Auntie Bert, was one of the best things that could have happened to Whitney. She grew up a happy, healthy young lady in a diverse neighborhood that believed in looking out for each other. During that time she didn't see her parents much but only questioned why, when she would see her neighborhood friends interact with their own. Her aunt Bert would always give Whitney the same answer when she would ask why she didn't live with her parents.

"Because God gave us both a present the day He decided you could come live with me." Whitney remembered her saying.

She never questioned the odd response; mainly because she thought her aunt Bert was the smartest woman she knew and could do no wrong in her eyes. So much so, Whitney wanted to follow in her aunt's footsteps, who was also a teacher. Aunt Bert's husband, Uncle Larry worked for the railroad and always made it clear that her aunt only worked because she wanted to. She could tell that he really wanted his wife to be home taking care of the house but that was a battle he had lost long ago.

Nevertheless, Whitney patterned her life after her auntie and uncle who treated her more like a daughter than her own parents. She often wondered if Levi could live up to the standards of a good man like her uncle had showed her with his many actions. The love Whitney's aunt and uncle had was the exact love she wanted for herself, unstoppable.

Whitney took another sip and started to surf the channels before she settled in on the VH-1 Network. Love and Hip Hop was on and she figured she might as well get her dose of drama in. The show served as a reminder of just how great her life was compared to some of the women on the show. After all, these women had fame, a little bit of fortune and twenty-four-hour access to a glam squad and still couldn't keep a man faithful. Whitney may not have half of that but one thing she did know for sure was her man was faithful and she felt blessed for that.

After watching Yandy accept another collect phone call from Mendeecees as he awaited his bail hearing, Whitney began to cheer up just a little. Of course she felt for Yandy's situation, no real woman wants to see another woman going through pain and heartache, but she couldn't help but be thankful it wasn't her dealing with it.

As Whitney engulfed herself into the show and all the drama it had to offer, thinking there are only so many collect calls a woman can pay for, she heard the door of her apartment open. She turned around to see her personal eye candy walking through the door.

Oh, yes, I would keep accepting calls from him! Whitney thought to herself as she watched him and his swagger in action.

"Hey baby. How was your day?" Whitney heard Levi ask, as he placed his keys on the hook located next to the front door.

"Baby, you don't even want to know," Whitney said, taking the last sip of her wine.

She reached over, set the empty glass on the table, and then turned to give Levi her full attention as he headed towards the couch.

"Of course, I want to know, otherwise I wouldn't have asked," Levi said, leaning down to give her a quick kiss on the lips.

"Let's just say, it's a work in progress and I'm not in the mood to talk about it," Whitney said right before turning his quick kiss into a passionate one against his full lips.

"Looks like somebody has some pent up frustration. Can I get in the shower first?" Levi asked in between the next two kisses.

"No, I want you right here, been waiting on you all evening!" Whitney softly demanded in between kisses.

"I have to keep my lady happy, right?" Levi asked, pulling her into his arms.

Those were the words Whitney had been waiting to hear and the arms she had been waiting to feel. She allowed herself to melt into the safety of both.

SEVENTEEN

Whitney was standing at her stainless-steel stove with her chocolate silk robe on, the belt tied tightly around her waist. She was listening to the cable music channel and singing along with Beyonce as she belted out the words to Love on Top. As Whitney danced around the kitchen, putting the finishing touches on the dinner she had started when she came home from work, she couldn't help but be in a better mood.

"You're the one...You're the one...When I need you...Finally you..." Whitney sang each verse into the silver spoon as she walked over to the dining room table.

Levi had put her mind and body at complete rest with no lingering thoughts of her stressful week at work. He knew exactly what she needed and never failed at giving it to her on demand. This was one of the many reasons she always made sure he had a hot, home cooked meal, and never turned him down when he needed her to take care of him. She had learned a long time ago that if you didn't take care of your man there was always another woman waiting at the back door to help you with your duties. Like Mary J Blige said, never let another woman cook in your kitchen.

Whitney was fixing Levi and herself a plate of lobster macaroni and cheese casserole accompanied by broccoli; with two half slices of lightly buttered garlic bread. Earlier when she started cooking she anticipated having dessert first, and once again she was right. After dinner she hoped they would watch The Best Man Holiday and Ride Along before calling it a night. If Levi decided he wanted to go for another round of dessert she wouldn't be opposed to that either.

"Baby you got it smelling good in here," Levi said, as he entered the room.

She could smell his freshly showered body from across the room and it was with the help of the Bath and Body Works scent, Nori she had gotten him for his last birthday.

"Well I made it just for you. Come take your seat while I change out of this robe. It will only take me a minute to throw on something," Whitney said, pulling the dining room chair out.

She watched Levi as he casually walked over towards the table. He had on a pair of jeans that hung grown man low on his waist and a black body t-shirt, both clothing items fitting his 5'11" frame perfectly. His arms were like mini tree trunks that made Whitney want to do circles around them like an Olympic gymnast on the uneven bars. His legs were the perfect complement to his arms, and a sight to see when he had on shorts. His sex appeal was off the charts and it didn't hurt that Levi looked just like Omari Hardwick, Gabrielle Union's love interest from the show Being Mary Jane.

Whitney knew she had to stay focused or their dinner would be cold if she continued to quietly obsess over her man, even if it was in her mind.

"Please don't feel like you have to get dressed for me. Baby, you can leave that robe on for all I care. You look good to me either way," Levi said, hugging her from behind.

"Okay, sir. You keep this up, you will get something started, and dinner will be ruined. Now let me go so I can put some clothes on," Whitney said, playfully pulling away from him as she headed towards her room.

Whitney heard Levi's laughter as she made it to her bedroom and she couldn't help but to laugh along with him, his laughter was infectious. She opened the third drawer of her beige oak dresser and pulled out a pair of her fitted purple St John's summer sweats and matching white and purple t-shirt. As she slipped her robe off, she heard the music channel go silent, and she already knew Levi was getting a song ready for her. That meant she had put something on his mind and that was a good thing. This was something he had done since their fourth date and she loved it. She could remember the first time he played her a song like it was yesterday.

"Let me play something for you," Whitney remembered him saying after he parked in front of her apartment building.

"This is not Love Jones. I'm not Nia Long and you're for sure not Lorenz Tate!" Whitney answered, laughing.

"I know that woman. Besides, if you were Nia Long you probably wouldn't give me the time of day," Levi answered, laughing along with her.

"So now you're calling me shallow? Tell me how you really feel," Whitney said, continuing to laugh.

"Okay, lady, all joking aside. I want to play a song that tells you how you make this guy right here feel," Levi said, pointing to himself, his laughter slowly coming to a stop.

Sensing the seriousness in his voice, Whitney decided not to make light of his questions any longer. She did have to make one thing clear with Levi to ensure they were still on the same page.

"That's cool and all but I'm still not sleeping with you!" Whitney said, with the same tone.

"That's fair enough," Levi said, before turning his attention to the CD player in the car.

Levi seemed a little tense as he pushed the button on the CD player. He didn't seem to be at ease until selection number five came up, it was like he found his comfort zone and was ready to show her another side of him.

After the intro of the organ and right before the drums, the first set of lyrics began to play a song Whitney had heard on the radio a few times. Levi turned his attention directly to her, his eyes fixed on her face, especially her eyes, waiting to see her emotions to his musical tribute.

Whitney listened intently to the rapper Wale and the singer Miguel as they belted out Levi's personal message to her. Her eyes couldn't help but fall on his as they both stared intently at each other while the music played in the background. She heard Levi's voice in place of Wale and Miguel, as she listened to the song "Lotus Flower Bomb."

At the time she wasn't sure what message he was trying to convey, she was hoping it wasn't sex because it was going to take more than a song for her to give that up. The more she focused on the lyrics of the song the more it sounded like Levi was trying to tell her he was falling for her. After the song ended they both sat there in silence for what seemed like hours until she decided to be the one to break the silence.

"Thank you for my song," Whitney remembered saying to him.

"Did you like it?" Levi asked as he turned the volume all the way down.

Whitney wasn't sure how to answer since she wasn't completely sure of the message the song was supposed to give her.

"I think I did," Whitney said, with a playful chuckle.

"That's alright baby. One of the things I like about you is your ability to be honest and transparent, no matter what," Levi said, then chuckled, before he continued.

"I'm trying to tell you how you have me feeling. I'm falling for you and I really want to keep seeing you and find out where this is going to go. That is, if it's alright with you," Levi asked, reaching over and touching her hand.

Whitney remembered being speechless, as she had never had a man express himself to her in that way. After she listened to Levi explain the meaning of the song and the reason he chose it, she knew he was going to be a keeper.

Since that day, it was as if the songs he had for her going forward solidified how solid his commitment was to her. This made her feel like the luckiest girl in the world.

As Whitney took her seat at the dining room table, Levi seemed happy she was now back in his presence. He said grace over their food before asking her if she was ready for her song. She happily said yes, while still remembering the many songs of their past. He always chose a rap song, which helped her remain in touch with what music her students may be influenced by.

Whitney was familiar with the song as soon as the cord began to play. If a person took the time to listen to the song "Power Trip," by J. Cole and Miguel, you would know it is an emotionally deep love song. Miguel had slowly become one of her favorite artists with the help of Levi, who was always playing music. When she looked over at him, he was singing in between bites. She was so caught up in the moment that she didn't notice the black box sitting in front of the black plate that contained her dinner for the night.

Before opening the box, she looked over at Levi who had now gotten up from his chair.

"I had a plan in place before I walked in the door, but you canceled that. So, I'm winging it right now. I'm going to put it like this, you know I have crazy love for you, lady and these past few years have been like none other for me. I want you to rock with me until the wheels fall off. Can you accept me for who I am for the rest of your life?" Levi asked, leaning down on one knee, opening the black box to display the gorgeous two-carat diamond cut solitaire.

Without hesitation, Whitney answered.

"I can't see it being any other way. Yes, I will rock with you until the wheels fall off, babe!" Whitney responded before leaning down to give him a kiss.

Dinner had gone to waste just as Whitney had predicted as they opted for another round of dessert instead.

EIGHTEEN

It was Monday morning and Whitney was headed to work in one of the greatest moods she had been in since the school year started. She had already given herself a pep talk before leaving the apartment and had determined to have a great day, no matter what. The first thing she had to do was not listen to all the talk radio and breaking news channels that normally filled her hour drive into work from the subdivision of Round Rock.

In honor of her new fiancé, she opted to turn the radio to the R & B station, something she rarely did, in an effort to channel positive energy. She knew the word was out about her new engagement because she updated her relationship status on Facebook the night before. She wanted to make sure she started out as upbeat as possible because she knew some of the women, especially one in particular, was going to shoot down her impending marriage before her engagement announcement could grow wings to fly.

As Whitney's Fiat 500c moved at a snail's pace the closer she got into Austin, she had to admit she enjoyed listening to her morning's new choice of radio. She couldn't help but be tickled by the Power People Poll Question for the day and wondered if the question was staged. In her mind, there was no way anyone would call a radio station and air their dirty laundry for thousands of listeners to discuss like an autopsy being performed.

The female caller was full of guilt because she had fallen in love with her baby daddy's best friend. She was hoping the non-licensed social worker's staged as morning DJ could help her figure out how they should tell her kid's father without anyone getting hurt. According to the distraught lady on the recording, she never actually cheated, but only started seeing the best friend while she was supposedly on a break from her now ex.

Whitney talked back to the radio and every caller that called in with an opinion for the young lady. It didn't matter that nobody could hear her comments but her; she still continued to chime in after each caller gave their synopsis of the ill-fated situation. Some callers Whitney agreed with and others she didn't, but it really did not matter to her either way, she was still reeling with excitement from the wonderful weekend she'd had. She was very thankful that for once her life wasn't the source of drama and quiet whispers.

Whitney took the service road exit and decided to take the city roads for the rest of her drive in. She made great time this morning and still had thirty minutes to spare. She figured the radio had something to do with that. Ironically, the DJ took a break from the reality drama and played the song Levi used to propose to her over the weekend.

Whitney couldn't believe she was engaged to a man she had prayed many a night for, a man that truly loved and respected her. In her mind, getting engaged would have been a much bigger event taking place at some highfalutin' restaurant with all of her friends and family secretly hiding behind a trapped wall that would collapse once she said the word *yes*.

At the end of the day Whitney had convinced herself that her engagement went exactly how it was supposed to. She had to take into consideration that Levi was not some high-powered broker who made bags full of money that could afford an extravagant proposal. There was no part of her that was embarrassed by him or the fact she made more money than he did. Her Aunt Bert always told her it was much better to have a man who worked a mediocre job, could afford to pay half the bills and treated you like their priority, instead of one who could afford to pay all the bills and more, but treated you like an option.

"When a man knows a woman needs him, he starts using cheaper bait than what he started out fishing with," Whitney remembered her Aunt Bert saying.

"What do you mean by that, Auntie?" Whitney asked, confused by the fishing analogy.

Whitney remembered her aunt having this discussion with her when she started getting serious with Roman Peterson, a gentleman four years her senior. She met him while a junior in college and working part time at Starbucks. He had all but convinced Whitney to stop working and going to college full time in order to travel with him and his job. He made enough to take care of Whitney, her aunt, uncle and still have money left over.

"All I'm saying is, don't give up your career for a man who makes more money than you. He can change his mind anytime he gets ready and where will that leave you when it comes to money? A man that makes a whole lot of money and don't have God in his heart is worse than a broke man who wears the same suit every first and third Sunday to church," Aunt Bert explained.

Whitney listened to her aunt's old school wisdom for what seemed like hours. Although at the time it seemed like a bunch of nonsense, she later found out her auntie was right. One semester she took all online classes and finally took two of the four weeks of vacation she had built up at Starbucks to go on the road with Roman. Under the impression she had given everything up for him, Roman slowly started to treat her differently. His money did not freely run as it did prior to her "being with him against her families wishes" speech she gave him when she came to his place a few weeks before.

It only took one week of his shortness of tone and especially his finances before she found her way back home. She spent her last week of vacation listening to Aunt Bert's expert advice on men.

"There is nothing wrong with having a man who makes a decent living, treats you well, but his income is not as much as yours. There is nothing like peace of mind, honey, remember that," Aunt Bert explained.

When Whitney ended her relationship with Roman, several of her friends tried to make her feel silly for doing so. She was constantly reminded of how many women would love to have a man like Roman and how his demands couldn't have been that bad. It wasn't until two years later when his mug shot was the featured story on the ten o'clock news for a violent assault and battery against another young lady around her age. She had never been so thankful to have listened to her aunt's advice.

After pulling into the parking stall that had a sign with the word principal followed by her name in front of the space, she gathered her black Michael Kors Hamilton Specchio satchel handbag. It was one of her favorite gifts from Levi and he even purchased the matching wallet and cell phone case to make it a complete set.

Whitney made her way towards the building as her yellow, white and black St Johns Bay wrap sundress with a water fall back swayed with the movement of her hips. With each step, her feet were slowly reminding her that the black wedge heel Michael Kors sandals may not have been a great choice. She was hoping she wouldn't have to do much walking today but if that failed, she knew she had at least one pair of comfortable sandals in her office she could slip into.

As soon as Whitney reached the building, she greeted the ladies that worked in the front office and headed to her own. She greeted the school nurse and a few teachers that were checking their mailboxes. Once she reached her office she unlocked the door, put her things away and turned on her computer. She walked back out of her door to retrieve her messages from the front. A few of the ladies congratulated her on the engagement as they admired her ring.

Whitney and the ladies were talking about getting together to celebrate her great news when she saw the one person she had said a special prayer for strength to deal with. She could tell by the look on Naylor's face that she knew of Whitney's news, even though she claimed she *didn't do Facebook,* as if anybody who did was beneath her.

Whitney refused to let anything, or anybody take away from the joy she had experienced for the past three days. She refused to let Naylor "the fake" steal her joy. She decided to do what every good boss, who was confident in themselves would do. She spoke first and made sure she had the best smile she could muster up on her face.

"Good morning, Naylor. Happy Monday to you," Whitney said, accompanied by a fake smile.

NINETEEN

Whitney refused to let Naylor mess up her morning, especially since it had started off on such a good note. Ever since her promotion, Naylor had been one of the worst to deal with. She expected the drama from a handful of the teachers but not from Naylor. The two had been really good friends prior to the job change and Whitney couldn't understand why. Naylor was having such a hard time adjusting. She actually let Naylor slide on a few things that she should have received disciplinary action for and one would think Naylor would show her appreciation by conducting herself like a professional teacher instead of a professional lady of the night with each male teacher she came in contact with.

Whitney knew she was taking a huge risk by having Naylor mentor Eddie, but she really didn't have a choice. She was the only tenured English teacher available for the task and the only way she could have excused Naylor from doing it was by voicing her concern. Whitney really didn't want to throw Naylor under the bus, although she knew Naylor wouldn't think twice about getting behind a big rig to run over her.

"So Naylor, how are you? How was your weekend?" Whitney asked, after Naylor's dry response to her greeting.

"It was eventful but certainly not as eventful as yours from what I hear. I can't believe I had to hear about my friend's engagement third hand. I thought we were better than that," Naylor responded, winking her left eye to complement the smirk on her face.

For some reason Whitney wasn't surprised by the passive aggressive response she received. She knew Naylor would not be truly happy for her, but she didn't expect her to show it in public, but then again, she did. After all, she was dealing with Naylor, a woman she knew all too well.

"I must admit it caught me off guard and I failed to *personally* tell several people," Whitney responded.

Before Naylor had the option to say another sly comment, Brazil, the new Assistant Principal came to Whitney's rescue.

"I bet it did, Whitney. At least it was a pleasant surprise," Brazil said, admiring Whitney's ring.

Naylor was so irritated at the sight of Whitney and Brazil; she left out of the office without saying another word to anyone. This behavior didn't surprise Whitney in the least bit, as it was typical Naylor behavior. Although she knew how Naylor was, Whitney was doing her best to be sensitive to her feelings. She knew it had to be a tough pill to swallow that she wasn't promoted, regardless of it being her own undoing and her pit bull in heels attitude.

Whitney exchanged a few more pleasantries with the teachers, parents, and students who came in and out of the office before returning to her own. Once seated in her black mesh chair, she slowly went through her phone messages and school reports from the day and week before. The one thing she was grateful for was the low rate of disciplinary issues she had to get involved in. She always tried to provide training at least once a quarter for her teachers and it almost always incorporated how to best de-escalate situations and keep control of your classroom. This was a training that Naylor rarely attended and if she did, she always had to step in and out of the session for one reason or another.

Whitney thought back to the conversation she had with Naylor in her classroom a few weeks prior. She tried to explain the difference between personal and professional in an effort to help her friend re-brand herself and get a more positive image out there. Instead, in typical Naylor fashion, she didn't take it that way and immediately became defensive. Instead of doing some soul searching, she wanted to remind Whitney of all the negative things she did prior to her promotion.

In the past Whitney never noticed just how evil and self-centered Naylor could be. She always took for granted that since the two had similar backgrounds they were the same. Whitney came to realize, that although she wasn't living a life of salvation she still had it in her. There were just certain things she wouldn't do, no matter what. Naylor, on the other hand, made you wonder if she ever saw the inside of a church or picked up the Bible at all.

When Whitney not only figured out the head games Naylor liked to play, but also how unapologetic she was for it and had no problem telling you, all Whitney could do was respect her. This revelation happened several months before Whitney was promoted.

Naylor was working overtime to woo Levi Hills away from Whitney, whom she wasn't in love with at the time, but nevertheless was crazy about. Whitney didn't believe it at first. She explained it away as both their imaginations that her good friend would make a move on her man.

Levi politely told Naylor on many occasions he was not interested in her and that he was into Whitney. Whitney wasn't sure if it was the thought of being rejected that drove Naylor, but she went after him full force. In Naylor's mind, there was no way he would want Whitney over her. At some point Levi was fed up and told Whitney what had continued to go on. Whitney was skeptical of what he told her, especially since they were technically on a break from each other at the time.

"Are you trying to set me up?" Whitney remembered Levi asking her over the phone.

"What are you talking about now, Levi? Set you up how exactly?" Whitney asked with much attitude.

"Did you sic your girl on me? Am I open prey now?" Levi asked, clearly mad.

"I'm going to ask you again and if you don't answer my question, I will hang up the phone! What are you talking about?" Whitney asked, irritation clearly coming through the phone.

"Bet! Did you tell your girl, Naylor we were on the outs? She has been blowing up my phone and inboxing me on Facebook, asking me if I need to talk. She even asked me did I want to come over to her place and it would stay between us. You playing some type of games with me or what?" Levi asked.

Whitney was stunned at what he told her and was hoping it was all a distasteful joke. Although she knew Naylor could be trifling, she never saw her giving her a dose of it.

"I have *nothing* to do with that and I'm insulted that you even entertained the idea that I did. But I guess that's another reason why we aren't together now," Whitney said before hanging up.

A few moments later a flood of text messages came from Levi. He went from cussing her out, to telling her how much he loved her and couldn't understand why she continued to push him away. She responded to a few of them only to further make him mad. He insisted that he wanted nothing to do with Naylor and had every intention of exposing her for the liar she was the next time they were all in the same room together. It didn't take long for the moment to present itself.

"I told my lady about the crazy stunt you pulled. I want to make something clear, I have a woman, and I'm not interested in you, have never been. Please stop calling my phone." Whitney remembered Levi saying to Naylor while they were all attending John Legend's and Tamar Braxton's concert.

"What are you talking about, Levi?" Naylor asked, doing her best to mask her guilty look.

"You know *exactly* what I'm talking about, Naylor. I saved the messages," Levi said, taking a sip of his drink.

"What messages? Are you serious right now, Boo Boo?" Naylor said, putting her hand on her slender hip.

Whitney saw where the conversation was going and also noticed that other concert goers were starting to take notice of the confrontation in the making. Since neither one seemed to be ready to back down, she decided to intervene.

"Baby, now is not the place for this conversation and I'm sure it's all a big misunderstanding. We can talk about all of this at another time," Whitney said, sliding her arm under his while gently kissing him on the cheek.

Whitney remembered Levi saying a few more words before dropping the subject. Naylor had that all too familiar smirk on her face. She knew Naylor really thought she had pulled one over on her, especially since she continued to engage in conversation with her for the remainder of the night.

If Whitney knew Naylor like she thought she did, Naylor wasn't the least bit concerned about a possible fall out. The way she worked, she already had a plan in place prior to even propositioning Levi. Naylor had no problem with telling a lie, no matter how big or small. She was sure Naylor was counting on her not believing a guy over her; therefore, keeping her trifling ways a secret. Whitney had to get a clear understanding with her friend.

"Naylor, I'm only going to say this to you one time and one time only. I reassured Levi you meant no harm when you threw yourself at him, especially since you know we are dating. You're making him feel uncomfortable, so this has to stop now," Whitney remembered telling her during their girls' night out.

"Girl, don't nobody want Levi's broke behind. I'm trying to figure out what you doing with him?" Naylor said, emphasizing the last sentence.

"What he has or doesn't have isn't any of your concern. Stop throwing yourself at him and please stop trying to down talk me to him. It's not a good look," Whitney said.

"Girl, bye. Why would I *have* to down talk you to get what *I* want? Have you seen me? Have you taken a good look at me?" Naylor said, looking into her hand as if she was looking into a mirror before she continued.

"I'm every man's dream and their woman's nightmare. Girl, you know how I do, boo. But, for the sake of our friendship, I will reassure you if it will make this nonsense go away; I would *never* do that to *you*. We're girls, and girls don't do that to each other," Naylor said, taking a sip of her drink.

"Unfortunately, I have seen you and I continue to see you. Trust me when I say, you *don't* want to see me. I'm not intimidated by your looks, Naylor, a real woman would never be. Remember that," Whitney said.

"Well, I would hope not because if you were, I would have to disassociate myself from you. I can't have weak minded females around me," Naylor said, before taking a fake call on her cell phone.

Whitney knew that was her way of dismissing her and at that point, she really didn't care. After that conversation, Levi never got another call from Naylor again. That let Whitney know that no matter how tough a game Naylor played, she didn't want to have Whitney as an opponent.

L. A. Logan

TWENTY

It had been a few months since the engagement and Whitney was feeling the pressure of setting an actual date. Most women wasted no time preparing for that special day that would be a year to eighteen months from the date of the engagement. Whitney, on the other hand, was not so eager to get the white gown, heels, and tuxes celebration going. She had used lack of time as her reason for not sitting down and seriously looking at a calendar but knew that wasn't really the reason for her lack of enthusiasm. When all the newness, congratulations, and compliments about her ring wore off, she had time to really think about the commitment she had eagerly agreed to. Her excuses of being busy worked for a while, but now that her school was on break for a week, Levi was pushing the issue.

"Hey babe, my sister said she called a few times to set up a time to meet with you this week," Levi said, as he sat down next to her on the couch.

"I know, I lost track of time. I will call her in the morning," Whitney said, not putting her book down.

"Baby, that's what you told me last week. I was hoping you would use a couple of the days you have off this week toward planning your special day," Levi said, now preparing to read the Sports Illustrated Magazine he had purchased earlier in the week.

"Baby, I know! I will call her in the morning," Whitney said, masking her rolling eyes behind the book.

Whitney was doing her best to wind down and settle into a full week of relaxation. The last thing on her radar was wedding plans. She had a glass of wine on her nightstand and was trying to put a dent in all the new books that decorated her shelf. She had planned for weeks to start the Pastor Black series by Kimberla Lawson-Roby and was determined not to let anything interfere with that. She had heard so many of the teachers talking about the series that she went out and purchased all of the books several months ago, even though she never had time to read them. She figured she could get at least three of them in during the week.

"Why don't you call her now? I know she is still up," Levi suggested.

Whitney was struggling to remain polite. If she didn't know any better, she would think they were expecting a child with the way he was rushing her to the altar. She didn't appreciate him low key forcing her to get the plans started and she decided to get to the bottom of his constant reminders.

"Baby, what's really going on? Why are you rushing me to make wedding plans? Can I just enjoy my engagement for a little while please?" Whitney said, now giving Levi her full attention.

He had a look of confusion on his face and that made Whitney feel bad. She immediately followed up her previous request.

"I can't wait to be Mrs. Levi Hill but I want my fairy tale wedding and that takes time to plan. So can you trust that I have a plan and everything is under control?" Whitney asked, looking at Levi who seemed to be processing what she had just said.

Whitney couldn't help but take notice of the hurtful look that had now appeared on his face.

"Is it money?" Levi asked, shifting his body weight as if he was preparing for a response he wasn't ready for.

"I can work extra shifts if money is the issue," Levi offered, now standing from the couch.

Whitney instantly regretted saying her fairy tale was going to take time. Anytime she alluded to needing more time for something pertaining to their relationship, Levi took it as he didn't have enough money to help carry the load. The last thing she ever wanted him to think was he didn't have enough money to take care of her.

"Baby, of course not. Money has nothing to do with it," Whitney said, standing and grabbing his hand.

"Then what is it? I know there is something that has caused you to drag your feet these past few months. You're not as excited about getting married as you were when I first asked you," Levi said, eyes turning red.

Whitney felt like she was going to get sick to her stomach. She knew Levi was right, but there was no way she could actually tell him that. She had to take the conversation in another direction and she needed to do it quickly. The last thing she wanted to do was start the weekend off with a fight that could make her week off from work unpleasant.

"A fairy tale wedding takes time to plan. I have so many ideas of how I want my day to be and I just want to take my time planning," Whitney said, now walking over to Levi who had made his way into the kitchen.

"Just tell me one thing. Will you have a date in mind that will fall within the next twelve months?" Levi said, grabbing her by the waist.

Whitney knew only one answer would be acceptable and at that moment she had to tell him what he wanted to hear.

"Yes, it will be within the next twelve months," Whitney said before kissing him on the lips.

"Baby, let me play something for you," Levi said, after reciprocating her kiss.

She watched him walk back into the living room and turn on the I-Pad they kept plugged into the sound box. When she heard the intro, she felt like the worst fiancée in the world. Hearing that song let her know her actions were hurting him more than he had previously let on. The lyrics to Musiq Soulchild's song, "Previous Cats" had a grip on her heart as they flowed from the speakers. This was the song Levi would listen to after some of their biggest fights that centered on his loyalty to her. He always went out of his way to make it clear that she was blaming him for past hurts that had nothing to do with him.

For the rest of the night Whitney did everything in her power to convince Levi, as well as herself, that they would soon be happily married. There were times when she did second-guess herself about Levi and what he brought to the table. Although he was a great guy with a wonderful heart, he still had a past that sometimes reared its ugly head into the present. She did her best not to focus on it because everybody had a past, including her, but she did a much better job of keeping hers in check.

Levi had a daughter with a woman who was still madly in love with him. Keitha was a baby's mother from down under and she took pride in making Levi's life as miserable as she could. The only time she didn't give him a hard time was when she was wrapped up with some other man or if Levi was giving her what she wanted, money. At first Whitney didn't let it get to her but the more she noticed how little money Levi had and when he started working part-time security jobs that all changed.

Whitney was okay with putting up with Keitha's mess because she knew Levi didn't want anything to do with her and it was all about his daughter, TaShari, whom Whitney loved dearly. She also wondered how quick Keitha would try to take him back to court for more money once they were married. Would she have to pay child support on a child that wasn't hers? Would she and Levi be able to afford a child of their own once Keitha was done taking him in and out of court, all because he didn't choose her to be his wife? These were genuine concerns she had and there was no way she could talk to Levi about it since he already felt like he wasn't good enough for her.

When Whitney's mind would take her down this road, she would think about the wisdom her Aunt Bert would give, most of the time unsolicited. Her aunt made love and career look so easy and it seemed she and her uncle hardly ever had disagreements. That was something Whitney strived to have with Levi, a drama free relationship, something she had never had before. Levi was so easy going about everything and always respected her no matter what the situation was. She seemed to be the one who blew everything out of proportion and had trust issues. Levi was willing to work with her through all of it, especially after he found out how bad her past relationship was.

It took some time, but Whitney finally calmed down and worked overtime to have a loving and fulfilling relationship with Levi. That included loving his daughter all while overlooking her ignorant mother. She was praying TaShari didn't turn out like her mother because that would be a crime to have two of them in the world.

Something else Whitney learned from her Aunt Bert was to keep her relationship trouble between her and her mate. This was even if another woman may have found her way into your man's reach. Another rule was to never argue or discuss your business in an open setting. She would say you never knew who might be listening or looking for a crack in the foundation.

"Women can be just like mice. If they can get their head through the smallest crack, there is nothing stopping the rest of their body from getting all the way in," Whitney remembered Aunt Bert telling her.

This was during one of the only times Whitney saw drama between her aunt and uncle. She would never forget the day when a strange woman showed up at her door claiming to be pregnant by her uncle. Her aunt Bert politely dismissed the woman away from her doorstep and made it very plain she was never to step foot back on it again. Later that night all seemed quiet in the house, which seemed to surprise Whitney. She was expecting to hear at least a few elevated conversations that night and she would have understood why. The next day she knew something happened the night before between her aunt and uncle based on what her aunt said to her. Whitney was convinced that whatever it was had to have happened after she was asleep.

"Never let another woman come and cause discord in your home. As the woman of the house, you check another woman's feelings, opinions and foolishness concerning your man at the door. If he messed up, that stays between you and him and nobody else," Whitney remembered her saying as she cooked her uncle's favorite breakfast that morning.

After her uncle finished his breakfast made for a king, he laid his black American Express credit card on the counter, kissed my aunt and thanked her for breakfast. He went in the study, turned on the television, and clicked the channel to ESPN. After Whitney finished her breakfast, she went shopping with her aunt and got everything she asked for that day. Never again did another woman show up at their doorstep with information about her uncle.

Levi reminded her of her uncle, minus the money. Whitney knew she had to either truly get over the money thing or give Levi his ring back and tell the truth. Whatever she decided to do, she wasn't going to do it that night. Instead she decided to make him his favorite snack and cater to his every need for the rest of the evening. She acted like it was the last time she would do these things, because after all, one of these days it just might be.

L. A. Logan

The

Gentlemen

L. A. Logan

Donavon

TWENTY-ONE

It was just another day at the office for Donavon as he finished signing another high-profile client for his employer. As he headed towards his office, he almost skipped down the hallways at the thought of the bonus check he would receive for the month. He had been at Markham Communications for the past three years and was on the promotion fast track. Pratt and Pratt Electronics was one of the largest accounts he had signed to date. They had over six hundred employees and Donavon was positive he would be promoted from sales to consulting after sealing that deal. He had been hanging out with a few of the guys who worked in the consulting division and they made the same money he did with better work hours and less travel time.

Donavon had made it to his small office when he felt the vibration of his cell phone on his hip. He unclipped his phone to see it was Naylor calling. He laughed to himself because if he didn't know any better, he would think she had inside information on when he closed major deals. She always managed to call with a financial burden before he could even think about what he would do with his earnings. He decided not to take her call until he looked at his sales schedule. Prior to talking to her, he wanted to find out when his next business meeting would be in Austin.

As bad as he wanted to move to consulting, Donavon knew he would miss out on the perks of working in sales. Traveling had afforded him the life he had become accustomed to and he had to ask himself if he was really ready to give all that up.

Donavon Austin was enjoying the life he was living. He was a successful, single black man who was able to get just about any woman he wanted. He was 6'4", weighing a fit 223 lbs. One would find it hard to stay fit with the grueling travel schedule he had but he always made sure he worked out in the fitness center of the hotel. He met some amazing women in the hotel fitness centers. Another great perk of his job.

Donavon was a self-proclaimed playboy who was devoted to himself, his career, and whichever woman he was looking in the face at that time. With him constantly traveling, it was easy for him to have a few different women without any of them finding out about each other. He had the perfect job that allowed him to live his life the way he did, no real strings attached.

His phone vibrated three more times before he decided to see who it was that kept calling. If it was Naylor, she was going to get a few choice words since she knew not to blow his phone up during work hours. When he saw who it was, he immediately took the call.

"Hey, lady. What's up with you? How are my people doing?" Donavon said, praying she hadn't been the one he was ignoring.

"We're good. How are you doing? You in town?" Donavon heard Annisa ask him.

"I'm good and before you ask, yes, I'm still getting my little man for the weekend. I should be getting out of here in the next hour," Donavon said, closing the door to his office.

Living a single man's dream did finally catch up with Donavon a few years ago. That provided him with a blessing, the love of his life, his mini me, Donavon Junior. When Donavon found out about DJ, he was in denial and worked overtime to stay clear of his future baby momma, refusing to accept he was the father. The entire time Annisa was pregnant he dodged her phone calls and surprise visits. She was the reason he had the job he had now. It was the only way to keep the peace and keep him out of jail.

Donavon met Annisa Morgan when they were both working in the Loss Prevention department at Walmart. From the first day he laid eyes on her he knew he had to have her. She had gorgeous dark green eyes that complimented her light cinnamon color skin. Her shoulder length auburn hair held the deepest natural waves he had ever seen for real hair. At first he thought maybe he was interested in her because she was different from most of the women he dealt with. She was a little on the green side and he loved it. She made him feel like he could raise her to be the perfect woman for him.

It took some convincing and a lot of money spent on secret dates, flowers, and shopping before he won her over. Once their romance got started it was hard to stop. Donavon knew he was playing with fire by dating Annisa and the risks it could cause at work, especially since he had seniority over her but he was not ready to cut it off. After six months of secretly dating, their co-workers were starting to grow suspicious of their *friendly* relationship.

At first it was hard for Annisa to hide her feelings for him when she would see him interacting with other females.

This started to be a daily thing since Donavon made it his business to hit on at least one woman during the day. This behavior led to a few heated debates when it was just the two of them in the office reviewing video. Annisa got hip to his game and started to give him large doses of his own medicine. Whenever he would try to shut down conversations she would have with other men, she would throw his own words back at him.

"Why you mad? You know it's just a part of the job. I have to talk to them to throw everybody else off of what you and I have going," Annisa would say when questioned about Donavon's male counterparts she would hold conversations with.

This went on for another year until things came to a head. Annisa caught him with another one of their co-workers one night and two things came to light that night. Luckily for Donavon he was at a hotel when the sparks flew.

"So this is your new job? I'm costing you that much that you're out selling yourself to make ends meet?" Annisa said, sitting on the trunk of his car as he and the flavor for the night made it to his car.

Donavon had told Annisa a few months prior that he was working a part time job in an effort to pay off his student loans. She was skeptical at first, but he reassured her there was no funny business going on and he was just trying to do what he could to make things easier for them in the future. His lie had finally caught up with him.

"What are you doing here?" Donavon remembered the girl asking Annisa before he had a chance to respond.

Needless to say, that was how the fight got started. That night Donavon learned that Annisa was no longer innocent and she could hold her own in a fight. After breaking the two ladies up and sending his date home in a cab, he went back to Annisa's place to reason with her. He wanted to make sure she didn't do anything irrational that would cost them both their job. After hours of talking she convinced him all was well and she would give him another chance.

A few months later she told him she was pregnant, and he felt the ground shift from under him. To say he was furious would be an understatement; he was hotter than fish grease and he had nobody to blame but himself. He was so angry with himself that he had nothing else to do with her and adamantly denied she was pregnant by him once the rumor mill started.

Donavon transferred to another store a month before DJ was born. He had no idea how bad he had hurt Annisa with that move until she had him served with paternity papers at one of the regional training sessions. She along with a few others from his old store were standing a few feet from him when the processors handed him the papers and clearly said the words *You've been served.* It took Jesus and all of his disciples to keep Donavon from going off on her at the session once he realized what the papers were for. He had to call his mom who had always been the voice of reason for him.

"But, mom, at my job?" Donavon remembered saying as his mom talked him off the cliff.

"Son, you did this by running away from your responsibility and hurting her pride. Even if you don't think the child is yours, you were having unprotected sex with the young lady, so you know the possibility is there. You should have worked with her and did the test together. I don't blame the girl, if I was sure you was the daddy and I'm not talking that Maury foolery either, I would've done you the same way," Momma Austin told him.

Donavon knew his mom was right. After going through the testing and the truth being revealed, he felt like an idiot for even taking her through all that. Just because he didn't know how to be faithful didn't mean he had to treat her like she didn't. It took a year, but they finally got to a place that they could be friends and co-parent. Donavon believed she was the one that got away and secretly hoped that one day they could be a family. He and Annisa both grew up in a two-parent home and they wanted the same for their son, even if it wasn't with each other.

"Make sure you're on time, Donavon. I have plans tonight," Annisa said, bringing him back to their conversation.

"I got you, girl. What are you doing tonight?" Donavon asked, silently chuckling.

He already knew what reaction he was going to get and he loved every minute of it.

"Uh, nosey. But I don't have anything to hide. I'm going to a concert at the church," Annisa said.

Donavon was happy that his behavior drove her to church instead of drugs and alcohol. Annisa had been actively involved in her local church and even invited him to attend a few times. By her extending him a personal invite, it solidified for him she truly had forgiven him for the madness he had put her through.

"That's cool. DJ and I might slide through there," Donavon offered.

Every once in a while he would toss that comment in not because he was going to follow through, but to find out if the invitation was still open. In his mind if she said it was okay, that meant there was nobody serious in her life.

"Well, our church doors swing on open hinges," Annisa responded.

That put a secret smile on Donavon's face. He continued to make small talk with his son's mother for another five minutes before hanging up. He pulled out his checkbook and wrote a check out for five hundred dollars. He put Annisa's name on the pay to line and then signed his name. He had already paid his child support but always gave Annisa and DJ a little extra out of his bonus checks. In his mind, if he could spend with women that didn't mean much to him, surely he could spend to make sure his son and the woman who took care of him had a little extra too. If Annisa was okay, then that meant DJ was okay, and as long as Donavon Sr. had it to spend, those two would be taken care of.

L. A. Logan

TWENTY-TWO

Donavon unlocked the door to his Dodge Magnum and placed his black bag in the passenger seat. He was able to finish up everything he needed and would have the next three days to himself and his son.

When Donavon started the car, his Hemi engine did a silent purr with the help of the special double exhausts he had installed. He eased the silver on black car out into traffic and his mind took him there. He was thinking about Annisa and the possibilities of them if he could get himself together. After a few more moments of happy family time, he decided enough was enough. He plugged his iPhone into his stereo system and started surfing his music choices. He knew that love songs were out of the question at that moment.

After a few more switches, he decided he was feeling something old but not too old. He decided on Z-Ro, *Let the Truth Be Told* CD. He figured he might as well get it in before he picked his son up. Donavon did his best not to listen to music that was too rough for his young seed's ears. He still remembered when he pulled up at his mom and dad's house playing Trae tha Truth's *Restless* CD. He was playing the song "Quit Calling Me" and was rapping along to it. He was angry with Annisa and was so caught up in the song that he didn't realize his mother was standing in the driveway listening and watching.

"Son, turn that foolishness off before you corrupt my only grandchild!" Donavon heard his mother say after making him roll down the driver side window.

"Momma, he doesn't know what I'm listening to. He is too young to understand the words," Donavon said, now getting out the car.

"A child is never too young to learn. I bet when he starts talking and repeating that filth you will believe me then," Momma Austin said, taking DJ out of his car seat and heading towards the house.

"I don't even know why you listen to that junk, you weren't raised like that!" She said before going into the house.

Donavon laughed at the memory of his mother's scolding. She always wanted what was best for her son and now her grandson. He lost the battle of convincing his mother that it was just music a long time ago. Now, he just respected her by not playing his rap music when he's in her or his son's presence. Donavon turned his music up a little louder when the song, "Respect My Mind" started playing.

He was into the lyrics and just about home when the music stopped, and the car's Blue tube alerted him he had an incoming call. He looked at his display and saw that it was Naylor. He decided to ignore the call and call her when he was on his way to pick up his son. He had a lot to do before picking up DJ and he didn't have time for distractions.

Donavon had already called his folks to let them know he and DJ would be in Houston for the weekend. Of course, they were beyond excited but he was sure it had to do more with the grandbaby and not him. His mother was crazy about her only grandchild and Donavon was pretty sure DJ had taken his part in the Will. He was ready for the three-and-a-half-hour drive, but was hoping DJ was too. He could be a cranky three-year-old when he didn't get a good meal and nap in and that made for a stressful drive. Donavon was really hoping he could get a jump on the Dallas traffic since it was the weekend and traffic was horrible on a late Friday afternoon.

Donavon took a shower, packed a bag, and was back out of the house within an hour. He called Annisa once he was in traffic to let her know he was on his way. After hanging up with her he decided to call Naylor. He would not be back in Austin until Thursday of next week and he was sure she wouldn't be happy with that.

"Hey babe! I've been calling you all day," Donavon heard Naylor say.

"Hey sexy. What you up too?" Donavon asked, now getting on the service road leading to Annisa's apartment.

"Nothing, thinking about you. You home yet?" Naylor asked.

"No, won't be home until next Thursday sometime," Donavon responded.

He had been seeing Naylor for almost a year and half and he had her believing his home was in Austin. He had been able to keep up this lie because of his job. She had been to the company condo he shared with two other men. Naylor was under the impression that it was his condo and he rented it out since he was never in town.

"That long! What am I supposed to do until then?" Naylor asked, seduction in her tone.

"I don't know. I'm sure we can think of something. Tango maybe?" Donavon said, with a chuckle.

"What's so funny and I already told you I don't like Tango, I would rather Skype?" Naylor asked.

"I was just thinking about when I first met you," Donavon answered.

"Never going to let me live that down, are you?" Naylor said, laughing.

The two met at Best Buy when she was trying to get assistance with a laptop she had purchased a few days prior and he was there meeting a potential client. As he waited for his client to show up, he overheard Naylor's conversation with the young salesman behind the counter.

"What do you mean I have to wait for another one to come in? Can you check with another store?" Naylor barked at the young man.

As Donavon watched their exchange, one thing was clear, Naylor wasn't taking no for answer. He could also tell that the problem she was having with her laptop had nothing to do with the manufacturer but more so with the user. He quietly listened for a few more moments before he decided to put the salesman out of his misery before she did.

"I don't mean to butt in, but I think I can help you with your laptop issue," Donavon remembered saying to her.

Naylor turned around and it was clear she was getting ready to bite his head off until she stopped in mid-sentence. Her body, which was once tense, seemed to relax and her tone softened.

"I'm sorry, are you a manager?" Naylor asked.

"No, but I'm the next best thing," Donavon offered.

After explaining his credentials for the next fifteen minutes, he convinced her to meet him at the Barnes & Noble that was across the street. He reset her computer and reloaded the software, then showed her a few basic tips for operating the laptop.

"I insist that you let me buy you a drink or something," Naylor said.

As they say the rest is history, here it was a year and half later and they were still playing the cat and mouse game. Naylor wasn't the only woman he dated but she was the only one he gave large sums of money to outside of Annisa.

The two talked on the phone for a few more moments until he was almost to his destination. He told Naylor he would send her money via PayPal by morning and she seemed satisfied with that. PayPal was the best thing that ever happened to a man like him. He could send money without the receiving party knowing his whereabouts.

Donavon liked Naylor, but she wasn't settle-down-and-make-a-wife material. She was somebody he enjoyed hanging out with and didn't require a lot to make and keep happy. She was beautiful, professional and totally in tune with her sexuality. There was nothing he asked her to do that she wouldn't do, which he loved. At the same time, all the things that he liked about her were the same things that took her out of the running of being his woman one day.

Naylor made it too easy and he knew she was very materialistic. Donavon was no fool, if he was broke and couldn't pay a few bills, she wouldn't give him the time of day. He respected her hustle and didn't mind giving her money, after all he did stay at her place when he was in town, so he was just paying for his laying. It was a win-win for the both of them, although he got the feeling Naylor was slowly pressing him for more—something that just wasn't going to happen. And the fact that he knew she wanted more only meant it was time for him to cut it off. He just had to find a way to get her to break up with him; in his past experience it worked out better when a woman broke things off with him. He hated being that way, but he didn't want to take another woman through the same thing he took Annisa through.

Seeing her pain broke him and tuned him into a woman's emotions, and he counted that as a good thing.

TWENTY-THREE

Donavon parked his car and walked up the three flights of stairs and knocked on the door. When Annisa answered the door, he smiled to himself. If only he could get his act together for the woman who just opened the door. There was no doubt in his mind she was wife material, but he knew he was still too full of games to try and make that move now. He had too much love and respect for her to play with her feelings like that.

"Hey, beautiful. You got it smelling good up in here," Donavon said, as he closed the door behind him.

"If that was a compliment I will take it," Annisa said, heading back to her bedroom.

"My fault, you look and smell good, Annisa," Donavon said, with a sly smile on his face.

"That's better," Annisa said before a knock at the door interrupted.

Donavon picked up DJ who had just run into the room. He hugged his son and gave him a kiss on his cheek while tuned into a male voice at the door.

"Donavon, this is my friend, Tyson. Tyson, this is DJ's father, Donavon," Annisa offered.

"Hey man, nice to meet you," Tyson said, giving Donavon the standard handshake.

"Alright, cool to meet you too, dude," Donavon said, struggling to keep his thoughts together.

Annisa told Tyson she would meet him at the car after she finished getting DJ's stuff together. Donavon ceased the moment to find out what was up between her and Tyson.

"What's up with you and dude? Is this your guy now?" Donavon asked, wasting no time.

"Hey, nosey. Get out of grown folks' business, please, Annisa said, gathering the last of DJ's things.

"I thought your business was my business," Donavon responded, struggling to sound nonchalant.

"Stop all that playing and help me get the rest of his stuff together, so we can go. You already have me running late," Annisa responded.

"Okay, but you know my momma already has everything he needs," Donavon offered before getting back on the strange man downstairs waiting on his future wife.

"But seriously, what's up with you and dude? I thought you were single and satisfied or single and sold out, or whatever it is you be preaching. Did something change?" Donavon asked, picking up his son's overstuffed green and blue bag.

"Really, Donavon? For the record, I am still single, satisfied *and* sold out. Pump your brakes; he is just a friend from church. We're in the Singles Ministry together and there is a group of us going to the concert," Annisa said, keeping her friendly tone.

"So, are the two of you dating? Why did he come to the door to get you instead of the group?" Donavon pried, with a slight chuckle as if he was cracking a joke.

Annisa stopped what she was doing to look at him as if she couldn't believe what she was hearing. He knew that look but didn't care at the moment if he ruffled her feathers. All he cared about at that moment was her status with the man who had just left her doorstep.

"Look, there is nothing going on between him and me, but even if there were, I think it is inappropriate for you to ask me about it. Trust me, I will introduce you when I meet someone who is on that level with me. Just like I trust you and your judgment when it comes to our son, I need you to give me the same consideration. I know you're getting it in with somebody, but I'm not all up in your business like that," Annisa said, with a slight smile.

Annisa always had a polite way of getting him told. Donavon took in what she said and decided to put himself back in check, since she had politely done so herself. He didn't want to run the risk of souring their relationship or any future chances he may have with her.

Donavon handed her the check and told her to buy herself something nice as they made their way to the door. Annisa thanked him and they continued to make small talk as they walked down the stairs until they got to the last step. Once Donavon made it to his car, he slowly buckled DJ into his car seat while discreetly watching Annisa get in the Nissan Armada that had more females than males as occupants.

As he pulled out of the parking lot, he couldn't help but wonder what he would do if she did introduce someone as the new man in her life. He always wondered if she had a male Naylor she dealt with whom she kept at arms length like he did. Naylor had no clue he even had a son neither did she know any other real details about his life. It was obvious the man Annisa left with knew more about her personal life than just an average guy would be privileged to know.

Donavon pulled onto the freeway and noticed DJ was already fast asleep. He took advantage of that and turned his riding music on and began to think, something he found himself doing often. Today's thoughts had him even more confused: Did he want to continue to be a playboy and keep Naylor as one of his favorite toys, or was he ready to throw in the towel and give his son a proper home with both of his parents there to guide him under the same roof. He was still building his brand with the help of Markham Technologies, a place he found solace in once he was forced out of Wal-Mart after the paternity test became public. Getting back together with Annisa was something he always felt he had time to decide on; with her they could build an awesome brand together. After what he witnessed today, he might just end up with Naylor and become a man with plenty of money but broke when it came to his love life.

Branded But Broke

Jerome

TWENTY-FOUR

After walking out of his attorney's office, Jerome tried to call Naylor once again in hopes she would accept his call. He wanted her to be the first person he told about what just happened to him. Once again, his call went unanswered and her voicemail gave him the standard greeting. He had been trying to call her for the past two days and she had not returned any of his calls. There was no way he could find a way to talk to her at the school since they were closed for the week. Jerome got in his Grand Marquis and headed home, forcing himself to let go of the stalker thoughts that had recently invaded his mind. He had already picked up his attire for the night and was ready to celebrate his recent accomplishment.

As Jerome merged onto the freeway, he abandoned the thought of letting go of stalking and dialed Naylor's number again, and once again she didn't answer. He had waited months for this moment and wanted her to be the one he shared it with.

Jerome was listening to The Dream's CD, "Love vs Money", which was a befitting title for him at that moment. While basking in his newfound joy, he was also filled with mixed emotions. Although he had taken the final step to fulfilling his goals by closing a major deal that made him the proud owner of a chain of cleaning companies, he was also hoping Naylor would be willing to take their relationship public. The only thing that would make the moment better would be sharing it with her, the woman he was secretly in love with.

In Jerome's mind, he was already in a serious relationship with Naylor and had been for the past year. Now, if you asked her, she would describe it more as friends with benefits, a term he hated to hear. Each time she would say those words, his blood would quietly boil but he would manage to keep it from spilling over. He was careful not to show her his true emotions for fear she would cut him off completely. Naylor would follow the statement up with him not having money and how he couldn't afford her as a girlfriend. He allowed her off-the-cuff comments to go in one ear and out the other in hopes of changing her mind one day. Jerome would just take all of her antics and the fact she had already counted his money in stride, knowing she would be surprised when she found out the truth about him and his bank account.

The smartest move Jerome had made so far when it came to Naylor was not telling her his real financial status. He might have been an easy softie when it came to falling for a woman, but he knew Naylor was a woman who kept more than a pocketful of men in her high dollar purses. He could overlook her past and accept her for who and what she was, but only if she was willing to give up her directory of men. He was ready to embrace Naylor with all of her flaws. He was sure it would come easy once she found out she could get everything she wanted from just one man, and that man was him.

Even if he hadn't just signed the deal of a lifetime, Jerome had done all right for himself. He actually was a blessed man when it came to his finances. He was already a partner in a small trucking company and the owner of Johnson Industries, a cleaning company he started with hard work and determination. Through this company, he had a contract with ten of the local banks and six small businesses. He had a nice little nest egg saved for a rainy day or that dream wedding ring; whichever came first.

Jerome's mother always told him he would never be truly happy no matter how much money he had until he made God the head of his life. He listened to his mother but didn't follow through on what she taught him as a child. He felt he was in charge of his own happiness. After having to be in church every time the doors opened, he promised himself that once he could make his own choices, going to church on a regular basis wouldn't be one of them. Now, he did still send his tithes and offering and would go on occasion with his parents, but he wasn't a faithful member. He used how busy he was as the reason why he wasn't as active as he could be.

Jerome initially started out working at the school to have extra money to fund the start-up of his cleaning business. With much convincing, his best friend Daelyn talked him into applying for a small business loan, something he was adamant he wouldn't do. His father always told him never to be indebted to anyone, even the bank.

"If you find you need a loan, pay it off as soon as you can. Paying all that interest is a rip off," Jerome remembered his father saying.

Jerome paid the loan off four months prior with the help of his job at the school. His original plan was to put in his two weeks' notice with the school four months ago, but couldn't bring himself to do it. He couldn't stand the thought of not seeing Naylor as much as he was used to.

Jerome's vibrating cell phone caught his attention and also piqued his enthusiasm, he was hopeful it was finally the call he had been waiting on. After looking at the caller ID he saw that it was Daelyn, and not Naylor. He did his best not to let his disappointment be evident in his tone.

"Where we celebrating at my man," Jerome heard Daelyn say with excitement.

"Man, I don't know yet. I'm still trying to soak it all in. Can you believe it, man?" Jerome asked, allowing excitement to take over, finally glad to talk to a live person about his achievement.

"Man, I knew you had it in you. You should have *been* made this move. I'm proud of you. That's why I want to know where we hanging tonight." Daelyn asked.

"Man, give me a minute to get my thoughts together and I will hit you back in about an hour," Jerome said, happy his friend wanted to celebrate his success.

"Now, if you hanging with your girl, who I haven't been deemed worthy enough to meet yet, it's cool. We can hang out on another day, bro. It's on you," Daelyn said, in a joking tone.

"Man, there you go. I will call you back in about an hour. But on the real, thanks for looking out for me, I appreciate you to the fullest," Jerome said between chuckles.

The two talked for a few more minutes before they ended their call. As soon as he disconnected the call, Jerome tried to call Naylor once again only to end up with the same result as he did the past several hours. This was frustrating for him because he knew she wasn't that busy to not take his call. He was doing his best not to allow this to ruin his mood.

He had envisioned this moment to go completely different than it currently was.

When Jerome pulled into the gated garage of his townhouse, he noticed his neighbor, Lovely, was arriving home at the same time he was. It had been a while since he actually saw her and was pleasantly surprised by her new look. It appeared she had lost at least twenty pounds and sported a new hairstyle that was a perfect complement to the khaki-colored business suit she was wearing.

"Hey, Juke! What are you up to?" Jerome heard her say.

He usually went out of his way to avoid her but decided not to this time.

"Hey, Lovely. I'm cool. How you doing?" Jerome answered as he got the garment bag out of his back seat.

"I'm good. Just getting off work. Ready to get my weekend started," Lovely said, slowly walking toward the entrance leading to the elevator.

Jerome slowly walked behind her so that he could get a good look at the new and improved Lovely. She had obviously stepped her game up since the two of them were an item. Maybe she took his advice and decided to work on her appearance and etiquette.

"Well, I have to give it to you, lady, you looking good. Whatever you doing it's working," Jerome said, holding onto the elevator door until she was securely in with her things.

"Why, thank you, Jerome. That means a lot coming from you," Lovely said, looking genuinely surprised.

"Hey, just being honest," Jerome said, looking over at her again, doing his best not to stare.

The two had dated for two years before Jerome ended it. He enjoyed being with Lovely, but she wasn't as lady-like as he liked his women to be. Lovely liked to party and she

141

loved to look the part. He never knew what color her hair was going to be from one week to the next and her apparel always matched her clothes. He did his best to work with her colorful personality, while trying to convince her that corporate America would never take her seriously looking like a bag of assorted flavored Jolly Ranchers.

"I know, if I don't know anything else about you, I know you will tell the truth, no matter how bad it hurts," Lovely said, chuckling as the elevator stopped at her floor.

"Hey, you make it sound so bad when you say it like that," Jerome said, chuckling with her.

"You know I'm just playing with you. I appreciate you looking out for me. Because of you, I got a promotion at my job. Maybe if you're not busy later you can come down so we can hang out," Lovely offered with a smile.

Jerome thought about her request briefly and wondered how many people would be there along with them. Lovely always had a house full of people drinking, eating, playing cards, dominos and just being loud, something he didn't always like to do. This was an every week thing for her and was what took him to his breaking point in their relationship.

"And before you ask, it will be just you and me. Believe it or not, I learned a lot from you," Lovely said, before the door started beeping a warning it had been held open too long.

"I'll call you," Jerome said, giving her the same standard answer he always gave her on the rare occasion they would see each other.

The doors closed before she had the opportunity to respond. Jerome was thankful for that, as he had already done too much by what he said during their brief elevator ride. The last thing he wanted to do was lead Lovely into thinking they could have something again, but he had to admit she looked like she had gotten her head on straight.

L. A. Logan

TWENTY-FIVE

Entering his townhouse, Jerome decided if he didn't hear from Naylor by the time he got dressed, he was going to do something he had never done before; he was going to go over to her apartment unannounced. He knew he was taking a huge risk, especially when one night she made it very clear he was never to come over without her permission. They happened to bump into each other at the Night Life, at least that's what he led her to believe, but he knew she was there and made it his business to show up. After talking for a few minutes she made the comment she would be heading home soon. He just knew that meant she wanted him to come over; otherwise, why would she tell him that.

"What are you doing here?" Naylor asked, clearly appalled by the sight of him.

"You said you were heading home soon, so I took that as you wanted me to meet you here. Did I hear you wrong?" Jerome remembered asking her.

"Yes, a personal invite! Unless I say the words *come over*, don't ever show up at my house unannounced again. Don't act like you don't know the rules Jerome!" Naylor said, with much attitude.

Jerome remembered apologizing numerous times while she practically treated him like somebody she didn't know. Heading back to his car he felt a mix of emotions, but the strongest was calling her out of her name, one that he fought very hard to suppress. He could tell she was expecting company by the familiar way she was dressed and the ambiance he noticed from the door. He too had enjoyed it, but not as nice as she had it setup that night. He almost waited to see who the lucky man was but decided against it. It was easier for him to think he was the only man for her than seeing the contrary to his foolish thoughts.

Shaking the depressing thoughts from his head, an hour later Jerome was dressed and heading out the door. When he got to the parking garage he saw Lovely was still at home. He made a mental note of that as he was determined not to celebrate alone. He was going to find someone to celebrate his great news with and who better than Lovely, if Naylor wasn't available. After all Lovely had something to celebrate as well.

As Jerome headed to the storage where he kept his well-kept secret, a BMW M4 Coupe, he had fully committed himself to going to Naylor's and letting the chips fall where they may. Either way it went, there was no way he was going to sit in the house alone, especially since he had a familiar fish circling his bait. After his earlier exchange with Lovely, she just might be what the doctor ordered for the night. Maybe if he was honest and upfront, there wouldn't be any hurt feelings involved if he has to substitute her in the spot Naylor was supposed to be in.

Jerome switched out his cars and headed towards Naylor's apartment. His common sense was trying to kick in but he wouldn't allow it. Why he was so fixated on sharing his news with her was beyond his understanding. He wondered if it had anything to do with the fact she reminded him of the one woman he let get away. Ginger Holloway was his world and when she died, he never thought he could love again. It took a long time for him to get over not giving her what she wanted from him. That was until he met Naylor. There was no way he could ever let Naylor know his attraction to her was mostly due to the loss of his former girlfriend.

Ginger had the same appetite as Naylor when it came to expensive items, but she had her beat in the humility department. Ginger never had a sense of entitlement and was always grateful for whatever he decided to do for her. Naylor was the complete opposite; she made it very clear that she was worth every dollar she could suck out of a man. He knew with no doubt that Ginger loved him unconditionally but at the time he was too silly to embrace it.

"One of these days you will regret the way you treated me, Juke," Jerome remembered her saying to him on many occasions.

"You need to get your life right, son, so you can see that girl really loves you instead of running around with all these women that just want you for your money," His mother even fussed at him.

The day Jerome got the call that she had been in a car accident will forever be tattooed in his memory. When he made it to hospital she was in bad shape, almost unrecognizable. His heart felt like it stopped beating for a moment. He was looking at the only woman who loved him unconditionally besides his mother. A woman who helped him and had always been there for him and now she needed help and there was nothing he could do for her.

He remembered trying to pray but nothing would come out and when he did manage to get a few words out, it seemed God didn't hear him. It was at the time he also realized that no matter how many material things he possessed he still didn't have God in his heart. When God didn't honor his request to save Ginger, he was never the same again when it came to love, that is until Naylor became a part of his life.

Jerome was now in Naylor's apartment complex parked a few parking spaces down from her building with a perfect view of her front door. He only had to wait ten minutes before she emerged hand in hand with a man he had never seen before. He could tell by her behavior she was really into the mystery man. She had never acted that way with Jerome, especially not out in the open. On the rare occasion they were out in public together, she would make him drive to the outskirts of town while dressed in a baseball cap or some other unrecognizable outfit. She would always discreetly survey her surroundings like she was ready to bolt away from him if she saw anyone who knew her.

After watching the two walking towards what appeared to be a Dodge Magnum, Jerome decided to call her cell phone at that moment. He watched Naylor look at her phone and then put it back in her purse. For a split second he thought about getting out the car, running over there and making her talk to him, but he had to remind himself that he was too much man to put himself out there like that. Instead he pulled out of the parking stall and made his way in their direction. He made sure his windows were down just enough for her to see the car and then see who the driver was. When his eyes met hers, he shot her a smile before continuing on towards the entrance of the complex.

Once on the highway, Jerome called Daelyn and told him to meet him at Night Life. Once Jerome hung up with him, he called Lovely and extended the same invitation. If he knew Naylor like he thought he did, she would somehow find her way to Night Life, and he wanted to make sure he was front and center when she entered the room. If he didn't accomplish anything else before the night was over, he wanted her to see firsthand he wasn't as broke as she played him off to be.

Craig

TWENTY-SIX

It was Friday morning and Craig was sitting in his office counting money that should have already been prepared for deposit. He was reeling off virtually no sleep after another long night at the office. Owning a nightclub had its perks but it also had its many disadvantages. Yes, the money was good, but his customers made him earn every penny of it.

Exhausted was not the word to describe how Craig was feeling. He had been up most of the night and had the same person as always to thank for that, the woman he could never tell no, Naylor.

Naylor had been in his life for over eight years and from day one his energy for her had been explosive. In his eyes she was drop dead gorgeous or as his students would say, she was a dime piece, a ten, and a five-star chick. Her feisty attitude made her even more desirable, which along with a few other things drew him in like a mosquito to freshly perfumed skin.

Craig probably knew her better than most men because he really took the time to learn her. He knew what drove her ambition and what made her tick. To the naked eye of most, Naylor came off as a materialistic woman who would stop at nothing to get what she wanted. She made no apologies for who she was and that made him respect her that much more. He was intrigued with the fact that she knew what she wanted and once her mind was made up, it was hard to sway her. He loved a strong-minded woman who wasn't afraid to speak up for herself. That was one of the main reasons why he continued to deal with Naylor. Even if their relationship was no longer physical, and no matter what anyone said or thought about Naylor, he would always have her back and consider her a friend.

After last night, one would think their friendship was on thin ice and he was hoping to dispel that theory as soon as he handled his business at the job. Normally when Naylor would have him up all night, it was worth his while, but this time was for a surprisingly different reason. Usually when she came to the club she played it cool. They would speak casually, and he would look out for her and whoever was with her that night.

Craig was no fool, he knew every time Naylor stepped foot in his establishment she was on the hunt, but she never openly disrespected him while doing it. Whatever man she may have picked up, she was careful not to do it in front of him. To him that spoke volumes as for how much respect she had for him. She never brought drama to him and that was why she could get just about anything she wanted from him.

On occasion, the females Naylor would have with her would get into it with some of his other female patrons, but Naylor stayed on the sidelines, allowing it to play out, refusing to get caught up in her friend's drama. She was always careful not to get involved, no matter who it was.

Last night was the first time Naylor was involved in any real drama at his club and he wasn't sure why. At the time when he intervened it didn't matter if she was right or wrong, he wasn't going to let anything happen to her on his watch. The one thing Craig was sure of was it had to be something pretty serious for Naylor to loose her cool in front of the entire club.

"Naylor, it's me, Craig. I got you, calm down!" Craig remembered screaming over the music as he grabbed Naylor by her waist from across the turned over table.

As people made a path, Naylor was still swinging her arms widely and screaming at the top of her lungs. One of his bouncers grabbed the other young lady who had clearly been the victim in Naylor's barrage of swings. Craig couldn't make out everything Naylor and the young lady were saying, but the one thing he understood was the gentleman who had come to the rescue of the young lady was the reason behind it.

"Let me go!" Naylor screamed to him, as he continued his efforts to calm her down.

"Naylor, it's me. I'm taking you to my office. Calm down lady, I got you," Craig recalled saying as they made their way down the hallway.

Once they reached his office Naylor struggled to get herself together while trying to stifle her cries. Craig could tell she was more humiliated than hurt and he knew not to press her on what had taken place. Instead, he drove her home in her car and had one of his bouncers follow him. Once she was in and settled he told her he would be back after the club closed. She seemed relieved that he didn't ask her any questions or make a big deal about her actions inside his place of business.

When Craig returned to the club he kept his ear to the ground in an effort to find out who was the young lady Naylor had the scuffle with. He already knew the guy was one of Naylor's co-workers and wondered what could have possibly happened with the three of them. He didn't want to believe that Naylor had anything going on with the guy, but he also knew anything was possible when it came to Naylor. Craig had rescued her many times from crazy situations and a few involved men that wouldn't take no for an answer.

"Naylor, you've got to stop playing with peoples emotions," Craig remembered saying.

"I told him up front what the deal was. How is it my fault he didn't believe me?" The last sentence would always be Naylor's standard answer.

He could never argue with her about that because he knew she was telling the truth. She had preached that same line to him for years so he knew she had to be telling the next man the same thing.

Craig finished counting the ten thousand dollars he was taking to the bank and placed it in the secured deposit bank bag. He then put another five thousand in his floor safe before placing four hundred dollars in small bills and change in a separate money bag.

When Craig reached Kris, his front bar manager, he handed her the bag of small bills so she could get all three cash registers set up for business. He was a little late but he was sure they could have everything in place before the lunch crowd started showing up.

Craig walked out the front door and headed towards the parking lot where his black Dodge Charger was parked. Once he got inside, he soaked in the comfort of his leather seat before starting the car. He looked at his vibrating phone and saw that it was Naylor. He decided not to answer it until after he finished handling his business. He figured he had another couple of hours of running before he could get to the bottom of what was going on with the woman who had the power to turn his world upside down.

TWENTY-SEVEN

It was six o'clock in the evening and Craig had just woken up from a long power nap. He had been sleep for five hours and that was four hours too long. He picked up his cell phone and put the footrest down on his recliner. There were six missed calls, two from the club and four from Naylor. He knew she had to be boiling mad at him by now, especially since he never did show up at her place.

After making the bank deposit, Craig's initial plan was to come home take a shower and a power nap before heading back out. While out, he was going to drop off a few checks for his various charities, swing by Naylor's and then head back to the club. After waking up on his recliner and realizing how much time had past, he realized just how tired he was, especially after being up for over twenty-four hours. Getting in those few hours of sleep were a must since he had another long night a head of him.

Craig took a long hot shower, brushed his teeth, and was dressed within an hour of waking up. Once inside his car, he called Tommy, one of his mangers at the club, to make sure everything was good. Tommy was one of the few people he could trust with his money. Due to his hectic schedule, Craig had to have someone at the club he could trust with his investment and Tommy was that person. He was cool, got along with the staff and took pride in what he did.

After talking with Tommy and telling him where the checks were for the new uniforms for the football camp, he called Naylor to let her know he really was on his way this time. No matter how much he cared about her, he wasn't going to let her, and her shenanigans disrupt the businesses he ran.

The Night Life Lounge was Craig's biggest investment but not his heart. Sponsoring football camps and giving back to the community was his heart's desire. The Night Life was just the investment he used to fund the many free camps he sponsored for low-income children. There were many times he thought about selling the club to Tommy but always decided against it. He had one of the most respectable clubs in town and although he trusted Tommy and all of his abilities, he didn't want to take the chance of the club changing into the opposite of what he started.

The virtual voice announced the incoming call through Craig's sound system as he came to a complete stop at the intersection of Second and Chavez. He was still downtown fighting with the weekend traffic. He loved having a place in Austin 360 Condominiums Tower, it was his way of escape with one of the best views of the city, but the downside was the weekend nightlife. Traffic could be bumper to bumper over the weekend and when the South by Southwest Festival was in town, Craig didn't stay at his condo. He would pay Naylor to let him stay at her place, sometimes she would be there, and sometimes she wouldn't but either way it was a win-win for them both. He knew she was always in need of money among other things so he knew she would never tell him no.

Craig decided to answer the incoming call, he thought it would be wise to do since he was running late.

"When are you going to get here?" Craig heard Naylor ask him.

He heard something in her voice that he rarely heard from her, desperation.

"With traffic, another twenty minutes or so. You need me to bring you anything?" Craig answered, moving through the downtown traffic, headed towards the freeway.

"Can you stop by 219 West and bring me Tilapia Creole?" Naylor responded.

"Are you sure, you know how busy they are?" Craig, not really wanting to make the stop but knew he would if she insisted.

"Yes, I've already called it in," Naylor said, not missing a beat.

Craig was slightly irritated but what could he do about it. He allowed her to be demanding toward him and he hardly ever refused her. This time would be no different.

"Okay beautiful. I will see you in about thirty minutes," Craig said before he disconnected the call.

After picking up Naylor's food, he made it to her house twenty minutes later. When he arrived, she looked a mess, he could tell she had showered and put on fresh clothes but still looked like she had just rolled out of bed. He figured the fight at the club must have really taken a lot out of her.

"How are you feeling?" Craig asked from the kitchen as he warmed her food in the microwave.

"Besides feeling like a complete fool, I'm okay," Naylor said, lying across her couch.

"Did you take the Epson salt bath like I told you?" Craig asked, walking into the living room with her food.

"Yes, and my body does feel a little better. It's my ego that is hurt the most. I can't believe I let myself get out of control like that," Naylor said, taking a bite of her food.

"Don't beat yourself up. It happens to the best of us," Craig said, pouring her a glass of wine.

As Craig listened to her go on about how shame she was, he tried to redirect the conversation with no success.

"So, what was the fight about? Why did you throw the glass at your co-worker?" Craig asked, ready to get to the bottom of it.

He wanted to find out what happened to cause the mini brawl to begin with. He was tired of hearing about how humiliated she was but he dare not say it. Craig needed to get this information soon because he needed to leave in the next thirty minutes.

"I was mad. Why do you think Craig?" Naylor asked with much attitude.

"Naylor, that's obvious by the way you conducted yourself in my place of business. Now, can you tell me *why* you were mad?" Craig asked, doing his best to keep his cool.

Every now and again he would have to check Naylor and right now might be one of those times. He was still a little tired and had a long night ahead of him. The last thing he felt like doing was listening to the same explanation over and over again from a woman who was infamous for playing mind games.

Craig noticed Naylor looking at him strangely before she got up and walked into her bedroom. He wondered if this was her way of dismissing him or if she was going to retrieve something from her room. A few moments later, she returned, looking flush.

"Are you okay, lady?" Craig asked, his tone softer.

Before she could speak, Naylor began to softly cry.

"No, I've really messed up this time Craig," Naylor said in between tears.

"You know I'm not tripping about the little dust up you had in my spot. We're still good, lady," Craig said, now sitting next to her.

"I know but that's not what I'm talking about," Naylor said, wiping the tears from her face with the bottom of her shirt.

"Then what is it? Tell me what's going on," Craig said, picking up her hand.

It took Naylor several minutes to get herself together enough to speak so that Craig could understand her. As she went into explaining why she acted the way she did, nothing could have prepared him for what he heard next.

"I had just met up with him and told him I was pregnant and before I could say another word he called me out of my name and told me I was just out for his money. After telling me not to contact him again, he left me in the parking lot. So I tried to call you but you didn't answer. I called Jerome and I explained what was going on and why I was so upset," Naylor took a drink of the bottle water that had been sitting on the table.

"After talking to Jerome he started asking me questions and the next thing I know he, too, calls me out of my name and told me I was a money hungry woman who couldn't be trusted. He didn't believe I was pregnant either. After he hung up on me, I started thinking about everything and I decided to go to your club. I couldn't find you and when I walked up on Jerome, I just lost it. I was so hurt and angry I just clicked," Naylor said, shaking her head before she continued.

"I just don't know why on earth this keeps happening to me!" Naylor said at the top of her lungs before crying uncontrollably.

Craig wasn't sure how to respond to what she had just told him but he had one question he had to ask.

"Do you even know who you're pregnant by?" Craig asked, disgust was very clear in his tone.

When he saw how Naylor looked at him, part of him felt badly but the man inside of him didn't care. He had paid for three of Naylor's abortions in the past and he told her he wouldn't pay for another one, even if he had to take care of the child himself.

Branded But Broke

Eddie

TWENTY-EIGHT

Surfing the sports channels, Eddie was enjoying his time off work. His cousins and a couple of friends were coming over later for a friendly game of dominos. It had been over a month since he had hung out with any of his people, so he was looking forward to some guy time. He had put all of his focus into his position as the English teacher's aide at the school and was hoping to join the faculty as a full-time teacher once he finished school.

Eddie had a full schedule, working full time at the school, going to school, and working part time at Sprint, he rarely had any free time. He did his best not to complain since he was just a few semesters away from being finished with school. His plans were to continue working at Sprint part time to help pay off his student loans.

He had just settled into watching the Louisiana State University and University of Arkansas basketball team battle it out in the playoffs when his cell phone went off. He picked up the phone and saw that it was Clarke, the young lady he had been casually seeing for the past three months. He contemplated letting the call go to voice mail but decided against it.

"Hey, you," Eddie said, turning the volume down on his sound bar.

"Hey Eddie. What are you up to?" Eddie heard her ask as he shifted his body weight in an effort to settle in on a few minutes of conversation.

"Nothing much, watching the playoffs. What are you up to?" Eddie asked, glancing at his watch.

"Nothing much. Relaxing before I go to the musical tonight. You sure you're not able to go?" Clarke asked.

This was the reason Eddie wasn't sure he should take her call. Clarke had been talking to him about the musical at her church for the past month, but he stayed clear of committing to attending with her. He told her he already had plans which was the truth but wasn't the main reason. He didn't know how to tell her he wasn't ready to be seen at church with her. As far as he was concerned, their relationship was far from that status.

E.C., which was short for Eddie Cooper was a one-woman man when he was in a committed relationship, but he wasn't ready to try love again. After getting his heart broken by Brazil, he wasn't sure he would ever be able to trust another woman again. After his relationship with her ended, he dated another young lady six months later only for that to end in disaster. After dating for a year, she was ready to start talking marriage when for him, she had just barely made it out the friend zone. Needless to say, their relationship ended in disaster and he felt horrible for entertaining the woman for so long, knowing he wasn't that into her to begin with.

Now that he had Clarke on the line, he was doing his best to keep her at bay, especially since he knew he didn't feel the same way about her as she did him. The one thing Eddie tried to do was be completely honest with any woman he dated. He never was one to play games with someone's emotions because he knew all too well how that felt and he never wanted to inflict that much pain and turmoil onto another.

Eddie politely told Clarke he wouldn't be attending the musical and reminded her once again why.

"Clarke, we've already talked about this. We've only been seeing each other for a little over three months. Technically, we've only been out on four dates, and I made it very clear I wasn't ready for anything heavy right now," Eddie explained.

"I know this, but I don't see what the problem is with us going to church together," Clarke countered.

"Come on Clarke, we talked about this. You know as well as I do if we walk into the musical together, no matter what we say, we will be considered a couple, not two friends hanging out. Don't play," Eddie said, doing his best not to get frustrated.

"I really think it's because you're still in love with her ex. The sooner you come to grips with that the sooner you can really start living your life," Clarke responded.

"You really believe that?" Eddie asked, chuckling slightly.

"Yes, and so do you but you won't admit it," Clarke said, slight irritation in her voice.

"Well, on that note, I'm going to get off the phone now. Enjoy the musical and I will hit you up some time tomorrow. Cool?" Eddie said, hoping she would agree.

To his surprise she did.

"Sounds like a plan," Clarke said before hanging up.

Eddie put his Android phone back on the coffee table and turned the volume up on his sound bar. He was determined not to let what Clarke said bother him. It wasn't the first time he had been told that and he was sure it wouldn't be the last time. He would be the first to admit he still had a soft spot for Brazil, but he wouldn't go as far as saying she still had his heart. She had long walked all over it like it was trash in the street and he hadn't forgot how that made him feel.

After watching the game and few episodes of Criminal Mind, Eddie headed into his bedroom to take a hot shower in preparation of the company he was expecting in an hour. While in the shower he thought about what could have been with Brazil if only she hadn't crossed the line one too many times. He had long determined that these fleeting thoughts were a part of his healing and not him privately wishing they could reunite.

After Eddie finished getting dressed and settling back in on his couch, his Android buzzed again. He was expecting it to be Clarke; it was nothing for her to call him back after processing something he said in a previous conversation and needing clarification on what he meant by it. To his surprise it wasn't her, but the woman who took up too much of his headspace to not be relevant in his life any longer.

"What's up?" Eddie asked after swiping the flashing green telephone symbol on his phone.

"Hey Eddie, did I catch you at a bad time?" Eddie heard her ask.

He wasn't sure how to respond to Brazil's question. Part of him wanted to tell her he was very busy, but the other part wanted to hear what she had to say. The question was why was there even a choice to be made? After all, this is the woman who single handily emasculated him and he still had not totally healed from it. He surmised it to him just needing closure, nothing more, and nothing less.

Turning the volume down on his 42" flat screen he answered.

"No, I wasn't busy. What's on your mind?" Eddie asked, ready to work towards closing the door.

L. A. Logan

TWENTY-NINE

Eddie glanced at his watch to see how much time he had before the fellas would start to show up. He didn't want them to arrive and find him on the phone with the woman he had sworn off a few years ago. There was no way he could convince them that he felt nothing for her if they knew he was still entertaining her calls from time to time.

Eddie had foolishly convinced himself that he could handle working at the same school as Brazil. Working at William Hall wasn't his first choice, but it was the best choice in helping him get to where he wanted to be. As soon as he was offered the job, he called Brazil out of respect to let her know. He remembered the happiness in her tone when he told her but also remembered the sadness that shortly followed when he broke the news to her that their working together didn't change anything.

"I still think it would be best if we just remained friends and for both our best interest, I don't think anyone at the school should know we have history," Eddie recalled saying to her.

"Eddie, that's very selfish of you, don't you think?" He remembered Brazil saying.

169

"Do we really want to get on selfish Brazil? I gave you *everything* you said you wanted and what did you give me? A broken heart and trip to the doctor or did you forget all that?" Eddie remembered feeling just as angry as the day he walked in on Brazil and her lover.

After Eddie reminded Brazil how badly she hurt him, she agreed not to discuss their past with anyone at the school. He knew it would be hard for her, but he refused to allow himself to care, especially after all he had endured.

Eddie brought his mind back to the present conversation and listened to what Brazil had to say. She told him that although it was hard, she was happy to have the opportunity to see him each day and hoped that he could forgive her for everything. She took full responsibility for the demise of their relationship and would give anything to take it back.

As Eddie listened to her, he couldn't help but think back on their relationship. In his mind they were the next power couple and there was nothing they couldn't accomplish, especially after he finished school. Brazil had convinced him that she was ready to settle down with him and leave her past in the past. He ignored all the red flags that something wasn't right and couldn't totally blame Brazil for everything that went wrong.

After meeting Brazil, he knew he had to have her. She was one of the most beautiful women he had seen in a long time. She reminded him of Vivica Fox and had a very sweet personality to complement her looks. After getting to know her, it explained the hard shell she had developed when it came to men. Based on the things she told him, he knew her ex had done a number on her. Eddie made sure to take note of everything she said she wanted in a man and a relationship and set out to give it to her.

Brazil was the primary bread winner after landing a great job at a private school. He was going to school part-time while working full time at the Sprint store. Between his school money and his job, he carried his weight in the bills but didn't always have extra money to give her the things she wanted. She always made it seem like it wasn't a big deal.

"Baby, I'd rather have a man who was pursuing his goals, treating me good and with respect than to have a man who could buy me the world and treated me like I was nothing," Eddie remembered her always saying.

Eddie took her at her word and never questioned it, even when she became distant and started coming home late. She always had a reasonable reason that would cause him not to question.

"Baby, you know how it is with these private schools. You have to attend all sorts of fundraisers and meetings. I knew you weren't able to attend because of school and work," Eddie recalled this being one of her many explanations for her disappearing acts.

Nothing could prepare him for the day he walked in on Brazil and David on the couch he had bought for her birthday. The two were so involved in each other that they didn't hear him come through the door. At first Eddie thought he was seeing things, as he couldn't bring himself to believe his fiancé was actually intimately involved with another man on the couch he had worked hard to purchase for her. When Eddie finally wrapped his mind around what he saw, he was filled with rage.

"Eddie...wait...please! Let me explain!" Eddie recalled her screaming as he had his hands wrapped around David's neck.

Eddie was so angry he didn't realize David was unclothed at the time. Once life left David's body, he focused his energy on Brazil, who was now running towards the door. Eddie flipped the couch and everything else that was in his path as he grabbed Brazil by the back of her head just as he opened the front door. He pulled her to the ground and straddled her. He was about to take his frustrations out on her when a couple of their neighbors pulled him off of her.

Eddie recalled looking around the apartment at the destruction he had done. He immediately left and went to the parking lot where he saw the same car with the same license plate number he had seen Brazil in a few weeks prior. He had asked his friend to run the tag number and had got the answer earlier that day. This was the reason he had come home early from work to ask her point blank what was going on with her and her ex. After walking in on the two of them, he got his answer without even having to ask her the question.

At the sight of the car, Eddie picked up the bricks that were a part of the landscape at their luxury apartments and threw them into the back window of David's car. Brazil was standing on the sidewalk yelling at the top of her lungs begging him to stop while saying sorry. Before Eddie could acknowledge her, the police were there and quickly handcuffed him.

While going through the court procedures Eddie vowed he would never forgive Brazil for humiliating him in the worst way. She paid for all of his court costs and eventually all charges were dropped. Since David refused to press charges, the state of Texas had no choice but to drop the charges. Brazil did all she could to win him back, but his pride refused to allow him to go there. He loved her and probably always will, but he loved himself more. Going through that with Brazil almost cost him his future and he wasn't sure he could take another chance like that with her or any other woman for that matter.

"Eddie, I guess what I'm asking is...can we try again? I was young and dumb and didn't know what I had. I've been dating but at the end of the day, nobody compares to you. You're who I love, you're who I want to be with and I'm willing to do *anything* to prove this to you," Eddie heard Brazil say.

He sat there in silence for what seemed like an eternity.

"Man, I don't know Brazil. That bridge is not safe to pass...I have to keep it real with you lady," Eddie said, not sure if he meant what he said.

"If you can honestly tell me you're no longer in love with me, I will stop pursuing you. But if you can't tell me that, then I'm practically begging you to give me another chance. We can take it very slow and it will be on your terms Eddie." Eddie heard Brazil say.

Eddie sat there in silence. Before he could respond he heard a knock at his door. He had let time get away from him and now his cousins were at the door. He had to end the conversation before he answered the door.

"Look Brazil. I need a little time to think about this. Let me hit you back up sometime tomorrow," Eddie said, rising from his couch, wondering if he was making the right decision.

"Okay, I can accept that. I'm just glad you didn't say no," Brazil said.

The two ended their conversation before he opened the door. To Eddie's surprise, it wasn't his cousins at the door, but instead it was Brazil. Before he could get the door all the way opened, she stepped in and immediately kissed him.

For the first time in years Eddie didn't fight back, instead he embraced the woman who had broken his heart beyond his imagination.

Branded But Broke

Daelyn

THIRTY

After popping two Tylenol for the pounding headache that had plagued him for the past two hours, Daelyn leaned back in his leather office chair. He had decided to rest in his office for the next two hours instead of going home. He had another emergency board meeting that he really wasn't in the mood to attend but had no choice. He along with the other members had to deal with another teacher who had decided to post inappropriate pictures of herself all over social media. He sometimes had to wonder what went through a person's mind when they treated things that should be kept private like it was a part of the right to know act.

Daelyn did his best to keep an open mind whenever he found himself having to make a life changing decision in such situations. He himself knew what it was like to be caught up in a situation that was not the best choice for one's life. He had just been blessed enough to escape any public scrutiny because of his poor decisions. He had to ask himself if his headache was due to his hectic schedule or the recent situation he found himself in. The more he thought about it, he wondered if he had become an unknowing participant on a new reality show featuring the school system.

Daelyn Murphy was a thirty-two-year-old Austin, TX native who had rapidly worked his way up the educational ladder. He was one of the youngest board members and one of the highly respected ones, too. He had accomplished many things in such a short amount of time and was currently being recruited by other school districts in and outside of the state of Texas. Many of them he had already turned down, but he was seriously considering three: one in Phoenix, AZ, another in Charlotte, NC and the other in Baltimore, MD. At first he wasn't sure he could leave Austin but after the weekend he had, he was starting to think it may be the best thing for him.

Daelyn's ringing cell phone reminded him that his headache was alive and well as it continued to ring until he hit the ignore button after seeing it was Brazil calling. He stood up, picked up his cell phone and walked over to the couch that was in his office. He set the alarm on his phone, placed the ringer on silent, set the phone on the table and laid down on the brown couch in an effort to rid himself of the headache.

Daelyn closed his eyes and did his best to relax and put the past weekend out of his mind. Nobody could have paid him to believe he would be a part of a bar brawl, receive a blast from his past and realize Brazil wasn't into him as much as he was into her. In his mind his life was too stable for so much drama and especially all at the same time.

When Daelyn finally got to Nightlife to find Jerome there with Lovely, he was very surprised. He was shocked to find out she was the lady he had been keeping under wraps all this time. He thought maybe his boy was only bringing her out in public because she had finally changed her appearance. It became even more confusing when Naylor showed up and started throwing glasses and anything else that wasn't nailed down at Jerome and his date. That caught him completely off guard, and by the way his friend reacted, he was caught off guard too.

When the three of them got outside, Jerome saw Lovely to her car and apologized to her profusely. He told her he would call her when he made it to the house, so they could talk in more detail. After Lovely agreed and left, Jerome and Daelyn decided to go to Old School Bar and Grill on East Sixth street. Once they arrived, they had a few drinks while waiting on an open pool table. While waiting, Jerome began to tell him about his secret relationship with Naylor.

"Man, you actually love this chick?" Daelyn recalled asking.

"Man, I thought I did, but I think I just loved her potential and she reminded me of Ginger," Jerome said, taking a sip of his Corona.

"Her potential? Ginger? Bro, what potential and Ginger was much classier than Naylor? I know you're not talking *wife* potential?" Daelyn remembered asking him.

The look on Jerome's face said it all for Daelyn. He could tell that Naylor had put her famous spell on his best friend and he felt bad for him. Daelyn wondered for a moment if he should tell his boy everything he knew about Naylor, including the fact that he had slept with her a couple times himself. As he listened to Jerome go on about how she really wasn't as bad as everyone thought, and how she was given a bad rap, Daelyn decided not to tell him everything he knew, especially about his escapades with her.

"Look Jerome, you my boy and it's my duty not to let you continue down this road of destruction with her. Naylor is not the woman for you, she is garbage bro, and you too good for that," Daelyn explained.

"But bro, she saying she is pregnant. I told her I wanted a DNA test but now I'm wondering if that should have been my first reaction after she told me," Jerome said.

"What? Pregnant? By you? Come on bro, tell me you didn't dip without the cap on, especially with her?' Daelyn asked, disgust evident in his tone.

"She didn't say. Or should I say, I didn't give her time. I hung up on her. I was mad because, all this after she sees me in my BMW M4 Coupe and I see her hand in hand with some other dude. Next thing I know, she is at the club going mad on your boy," Jerome said, signaling the waitress for another beer.

"All the more reason you need to distance yourself from her, bro. She might not be pregnant, might be running a scam for some money. You know she money hungry, but you know what, tonight is not about Naylor, it's about you. We celebrating your success tonight," Daelyn remembered saying before they made their way over to the open pool table.

That night when Daelyn made it home, he had a visitor waiting on him. Someone he hadn't seen in three years, someone he wasn't too eager to have in his company—that is until he saw her sitting on his love seat once he entered his condo. The last time he saw Brandi Ives was when she refused his marriage proposal because she was still trying to find herself. That night he was devastated and didn't know if his heart would ever recover.

THIRTY-ONE

Brandi was the only woman he had ever loved and after he removed the dagger she left in his heart, he didn't think he could ever love again. He masked his hurt in all the name brand material things he could afford and went through women like they were dirty cars and he was a car wash. As far as he was concerned, every woman was just like Brandi and because of that, nobody could get that close to his heart again.

Daelyn and Brandi were high school sweethearts who had survived many relationship challenges over the years. When they both went to separate states for college they made a conscience decision to end their relationship until they finished school. They both agreed it would be too much pressure to have a long-distance relationship and concentrate on school. Although they were not officially a couple, they still remained close and saw each other over the holiday and school breaks. In Daelyn's mind they became closer than ever so when he proposed two years after they graduated from college and being back together, he thought it was a no brainier.

"What are you doing?" Daelyn remembered Brandi asking.

"What does it look like I'm doing?" Daelyn answered.

He would always remember that day. It was the weekend before Thanksgiving and they were preparing to visit their parents in San Antonio. He thought it would be good to ask beforehand and they tell their parents together and what better time to do it but over Thanksgiving. He was sadly mistaken.

"Baby, you know things haven't been exactly perfect with us," He remembered Brandi saying, not able to look him in the eye.

Daelyn knew they had been arguing a little more than normal about money, but he figured that was normal for couples. She was spending money on name brand clothes, shoes, purses, and accessories faster than they could make it. He was trying to put her on a budget and she didn't want any parts of it.

"Bae, we've been arguing about money, what couple doesn't? Surely that can't be the reason why you're not saying yes?" Daelyn recalled asking her.

He got up off one knee and was now looking down at her confused looking face.

"I love you, God knows I do…but…I…I need more time. We're still young…I need more time," Brandi said.

"More time for what?" Daelyn asked, doing his best to mask his hurt.

"I need time to find myself Daelyn. I need to figure out who I am and what I really want to do with my life. I hope you can understand that," Daelyn remembered Brandi saying those words to him in a matter of fact tone.

That Thanksgiving was the last holiday the two spent together. He came home a week later to a Dear John note. He tried to call Brandi several times and never received a return phone call. After a few months, he gave up and decided to move on with his life. That's when he picked up his desire for the finer things in life and also when he became a serial dater. A few months later is when he met Brazil who was like a breath of fresh air compared to the women he had been dating.

Back then he refused to let anyone in until he met Brazil, she could have had his heart had she wanted it. She let him know early on that she was not looking for anything heavy although she treated him like he was the only man she wanted. He followed her lead in hopes of not prematurely falling for another woman who wasn't ready for the love he had to offer.

Daelyn's alarm went off reminding him he had a meeting to attend in forty-five minutes and he needed to get up. When he sat up on the couch he realized his headache had all but dissipated. He was thankful for that and was hoping the meeting wouldn't last longer than a couple of hours. He was ready to go home and handle the situation he had waiting on him. Brandi had been at his house the entire weekend and he was trying to figure out what he was going to do.

"*How* did you get in here?" Daelyn remembered asking Brandi after he got home from hanging out with Jerome.

"I used my key. I'm shocked you didn't get the locks changed," Brandi responded.

"Okay, *what* are you doing here?" Daelyn recalled asking.

"Daelyn, take a deep breath before you blow a gasket," Brandi responded.

Daelyn remembered closing the door behind him and sitting his phone, wallet and keys on the living room table. He took a deep breath as Brandi instructed before saying his next words.

"*What* do you want from me, Brandi?" He recalled asking.

"Just you for starters. I know this is selfish of me but since you're being direct, I guess I need to be as well," Brandi said.

Daelyn remembered sitting there, silent while taking in everything Brandi had to say. As he listened, in his heart of hearts he couldn't deny that he was happy to see her and to know that she was professing to have never gotten over him. He took in every word she said while discreetly looking her over. She always reminded him of Janet Jackson with her looks and her body. She still looked beautiful to him and he still had that same heart connection with her.

They sat and talked for a few hours while he ignored his vibrating phone. It wasn't long before they got fully reacquainted and again, it was as if they never missed a beat. The passion they shared made it clear they missed each other, and their hearts were still in it.

It wasn't until the next morning that Daelyn discovered Brandi had answered his phone when Brazil called.

"What are you talking about?" Daelyn recalled asking Brazil.

"I called you earlier and your ex answered. She said you were in the shower and would have you call me back. So again, I will ask, when were you going to tell me you two were back together?" Brazil asked, voice calm.

"It actually just happened last night and I'm not sure what we are doing. Can we meet for lunch so we can talk about it?" Daelyn asked.

He wasn't prepared for what Brazil had to say.

"I honestly think things happen for a reason and we were to only be for a season but were pushing for more," Brazil said.

Daelyn remembered taking a seat on one of the bar stools in his kitchen while watching Brandi cook breakfast for him while wearing one of his t-shirts.

"What do you mean by that exactly?" He asked Brazil, feeling conflicted.

"You and I know that we were trying to force something that wasn't there. I think that because our hearts were someplace else, we could never get it right. Let's follow our hearts and see where it takes us. If we find our way back to each other then we know what we need to do. If we don't find our way back then we know what was really meant to be," Brazil said.

Daelyn was somewhat surprised by how calm she was while discussing the fate of their relationship.

"Are you sure you don't want to have lunch? I really would like to discuss this face to face," Daelyn asked still feeling conflicted.

"No Daelyn. I think we both need to work on mending our hearts that have been broken for far too long now. Time to live in our reality, my dear. No matter what, we will always be friends," Brazil said, slightly chuckling.

He was still a little surprised but wasn't shocked. He knew Brazil was still in love with her ex. Not because she told him directly but because she talked in her sleep. She was always saying his name while sleeping. At first he would say something to her but then decided to let it go once he realized he was still fighting his own demons when it came to his ex. Reluctantly, he agreed with Brazil's suggestion and wished her the best. He also made it very clear that he considered her a very dear friend, and he would do anything he could for her. He could tell by the look on Brandi's face she wasn't too happy with his statement but in that moment he didn't care. He wanted to make sure it was clear Brazil was not his enemy, but the woman who helped him feel loved again and for that he would always be grateful.

Right before going into his meeting, Daelyn called Brandi to let her know what time he would be home. He decided to take a chance on love with her one more time. Maybe they could get a fresh start in one of the cities that had been courting him. He wasn't sure if staying in Austin would be the best choice in their quest to start anew. The one thing he knew for sure was failure wasn't an option. If it didn't work this time with Brandi, he was going to wave the white flag on love and not give it another chance for a while. It was either that or take a chance on being the agenda item of an emergency board meeting.

THIRTY-TWO

It had been another long week at the office and Darrel was ready to get the vacation he had been planning for months started. He had worked overtime to tie up all possible loose ends, since his communication would be limited while he was out. He and Layla were going on a seven-day cruise and he was not committing to checking his email several times a day. He would have the city paid cell phone with him for true emergencies, but he was praying it wouldn't be necessary.

Darrel had successfully briefed his office on the continued controversy surrounding how the state of Texas executed inmates who were on death row. The situation had made national news. Reporters from all over the United States were in the city of Austin in preparation for the court hearings that would decide the fate of an inmate's life. The fact that the court proceedings were being held in his city made him unsure key staff were trained on how to answer any questions that may be directed to their office. The last thing he needed was an unauthorized statement being released that would cause negative backlash on his watch.

Darrel left his office and headed to the parking deck where his Infinity QX80 was parked in his assigned parking stall. He had to make a couple of stops before he picked Layla up to begin their three-hour journey to Galveston, TX so they could board the boat. He had high hopes for this trip and he wanted everything to be perfect for Layla, for them. He felt it was time for them to take their almost three-year relationship to another level and what better way to start than on a romantic cruise.

Darrel Woods believed in the institution of marriage as long as it was with someone he was compatible with. Being raised by both his parents who showed him what healthy love looked like only made him want it more, but he was never in a hurry. His dad always told him to make sure he was together as a man before he tried to attach someone to himself.

"Son, it's much harder to get yourself together spiritually, mentally, and financially if you've already created a family for yourself. Take your time and grow into the man God intends for you to be before you find a wife and start a family," Darrel remembered his father telling him.

Whenever his mother saw him getting too close to the wrong one she would let him know and made no apologizes for it.

"Son, she is not the one for you. Her motives aren't pure," He recalled his mother saying on a few occasions.

At first Darrel would try to negotiate with his mother in an effort to find fault in her conclusion about the young ladies she spoke the negative expectation over, but eventually he stopped. His mother had so far been correct, and he was thankful he took heed to what she had to say.

Darrel was raised a Church of God in Christ boy and he credited his raising in making him the man he had become. He didn't always get it right in life, but he never strayed too far from what he was raised to believe in. He was willing to bet his savings account that being made to attend Sunshine Band, Purity Classes and countless Auxiliaries in Ministries services and conventions played a major role in keeping him grounded. Now he was a successful black man who had not seen the inside of a prison, had no children, and had a moral compass that still worked, all of this at the age of thirty-two.

Now that he had his life in order he was ready to add to his life, he was ready to have that wife his father and mother had been preparing him for the past several years. Layla had passed all natural and spiritual tests his mother had put her through. The fact his mother spent quality time with Layla and they also attended church together earned Layla a guarantee place in his family. Even if for some reason they didn't end up together, he was positive his mother would still welcome Layla over for the holidays.

Darrel also got along well with Layla's family. If he didn't think it would cause a problem, he would send Kelvin a thank you card. Based off all he knew about him, he would make a drug addict look like a saint when compared to him. Kelvin did a lot of damage to Layla with his actions and Darrel could never understand how Kelvin could treat Layla in such away. She was one of the most beautiful, caring, giving and loving women he had ever met. Loving her was easy, even with the flaws she did have, falling in love with her seemed effortlessly. The twenty percent she didn't have, he could live without it for the rest of his life if it meant he could have the eighty percent she did have.

Now that Darrel had found the one, he wanted to make sure he did everything right when it came to their relationship. They had crossed the line of sex early on in their relationship but had stopped the act all together three months ago. This came into play at the suggestion of Layla, which made him feel bad.

"Darrel, now that I've been going to church with your mom, I really don't feel comfortable getting it in with you. I think we need to try and cool it until we figure out exactly where our relationship is going," He remembered her saying over dinner one night.

"Or you can stop going to church with my mother," Darrel said in a joking tone.

He was glad that Layla laughed because he really didn't like heavy conversations.

"Darrel, stop it. I'm being serious, silly. Now that I have more of an understanding of the Bible for myself, I think we need to cease and desist with our sex life, babe. Sex can cloud things, don't you agree?" Layla asked before taking a bite of her food.

Darrel recalled studying her while she talked and watched her body language. He had to make sure this wasn't a topic of conversation because she wasn't happy or had started stepping out on him. After healthy back and forth dialogue, they agreed to no sex for at least the next three months. So far it had worked out great and made them closer than ever.

He was hoping she didn't think he expected sex during the cruise since the three months would be up while they were on the boat. Darrel truly wouldn't have a problem with them waiting another three months, if it continued to positively grow the two of them in the areas that were needed. Because of the love he had for her, he would do whatever she was comfortable with but was praying she would want to wait. By doing so, this would show him they were on the same page spiritually and that would make their vacation time together significant in his eyes.

Darrel had made it to his bank with time to spare. Once inside, he let the young lady at the customer service desk know he needed to get into his safety deposit box. She asked him for his identification and had him sign the necessary logbook before asking him to have a seat in the vault waiting area. After waiting a few minutes a gentleman approached him, asked to see his identification again and then escorted him to the vault that contained his many safety deposit boxes.

He opened the one that contained the four-carat diamond engagement ring he had purchased for Layla two months ago. He had planned to ask her back then but didn't want her to think he was only doing it because they had stopped having premarital sex. She had only been the second woman he could say he loved but the first he would present a ring to. He wanted the timing to be just right, unlike how it was for him and Imani Washington, the woman who first won his heart.

Darrel and Imani grew up in church together and she was his first taste of love, but someone else may call it puppy love. He and Imani got along well and seemed to have the same values and goals when it came to life. They started dating after her parents asked his parents if Darrel could escort her to the prom. He was so happy they said yes, he could hardly contain his excitement. She was considered one of the most beautiful girls in his church and the fact that she was very intelligent made her a hot commodity. Her persona was that of a super model, who required more than the average man could afford. He was willing to break his back to keep her and make her happy. Darrel's mother let it be known from day one that she wasn't fond of the courtship.

"Son, she will break your heart as soon as she leaves for college," He recalled his mother saying.

"Mom, I don't think she would do that. Imani and I are really good friends and I know she wouldn't do that to me."

"Son, that little girl already has her nose in the air and I can't half blame her. That's the type of household she grew up in and how her parents have raised her to be. You will *never* be good enough for her and will never make enough money to keep a spirit like that happy."

Darrel heard his mom say this to him many times until the week he was getting ready to leave for college. He had spent all his free time between work and church with Imani because it would be at least a month before they saw each other again. He could tell his mother wasn't happy about it and she finally broke her silence.

"I'm going to keep quiet about Imani. You're eighteen now, getting ready for college and I'm not going to always be there to protect you from these Jezebel and Delilah spirits. I just have to pray that you will allow God to guide you," Darrel remembered those words like they were just said to him on yesterday.

It didn't take long for everything his mother said to come to fruition and just like she said, it did hurt. It was hurt he wouldn't wish on his worst enemy, but it was a hurt that allowed him to be compassionate toward Layla. He saw the same garment of hurt on her that he once wore, and he believed in his heart that God allowed him to go through all of the hurt and pain to be the covering Layla needed. For that he was grateful.

Branded But Broke

Darrel

THIRTY-THREE

Darrel left the bank with the ring and two thousand dollars in cash. He then headed to Layla's place to pick her up. He was nervous but to his surprise he was in a great mood. In the back of his mind he wondered what he would do if by chance Layla told him no. Nobody wanted to be rejected and Darrel was no exception. He had been rejected before by a woman he loved, unconditionally, and that was something he didn't want to experience again.

"What was that about?" Darrel recalled asking Imani while showing her a Facebook post that had been forwarded to him.

"I don't know what you mean Darrel. What is what?" Imani was very nonchalant about the information concerning her on social media.

"Who is the guy that has showed up at your door three times in less than an hour now?" Darrel was beyond irritated with the mind games Imani had been playing with him over the past month and a half.

He had surprised her by showing up at her campus, unannounced, in hopes to spending some quality time with the love of his life. Ironically, while there, one of his friends that attended school with Imani saw him at the gas station.

After finding out Darrel was there to see Imani, he told him he thought they had broken up. By the end of their conversation the guy filled him in on everything Imani had been doing while away at school. He even had Facebook posts to back up his claims against Imani.

At first Darrel didn't believe it since he had never seen anything questionable on her page. After he figured out she had her page set to where he, along with anybody who knew him, couldn't see certain things posted by certain people, he knew the claims had some merit. This information sent him into a tailspin. He didn't want to believe that the Imani he knew would disrespect him in such away.

Darrel had to admit to himself that he had purposely missed some signs that Imani wasn't being forthright with him, but he dare not say anything to her. He was hoping whatever trip Imani was on they could work it out, but that changed when he saw the messages for himself. Gregory Wilson, whoever he was, apparently had his girlfriend's full attention by way of the social media messages he saw. He wondered if this was the guy who kept coming to her room.

"He is my *friend*, Darrel. Don't you have *friends* on campus that are females?" Imani asked, and Darrel knew she was trying to flip the conversation like she had done in the past, but today it wasn't going to work.

"Not *friends* who would disrespect you if you were at my place," Before Darrel could finish the rest of his thought, there was another knock on the door.

Imani's demeanor quickly changed from semi-relaxed to a slight panic as she made her way back to the door. Darrel heard a few words she exchanged with the gentleman, and it seemed like he was upset. When Darrel made his way to the living room, he saw Imani and her *friend* bring in two baskets of her clothes, shoes and jewelry. Before her friend left, he told her not to call him anymore until she was ready to stop playing games. This infuriated Darrel, but he wasn't sure who it should be directed to, especially since the guy never acknowledged his presence.

"Imani, what is going on? Have you been staying with this guy? Who is he to you?" Darrel couldn't get all of his questions and thoughts out before she had an outburst.

"Darrel, I can't do this anymore! I need you to leave, please!" He remembered her saying.

"What?" Her statement confused Darrel as he was expecting an explanation not a dismissal.

"You heard me. I want you to leave, please," Imani said, walking towards her front door.

"Okay, but what did I do to you that I'm being asked to leave? Can I get an explanation as to what is going on? You owe me that Imani," Darrel remembered asking while he gathered his things.

He had just paid half her rent and provided her with spending money, something he had been doing for a while.

"Okay, you're right, where are my manners," She said in a sarcastic tone.

"Here's the thing, this long distant relationship isn't working for me anymore. I need more than what you are able to give me," Imani suddenly had a severe attitude.

"I appreciate everything you've done for me, but you don't make me happy anymore, Darrel. You're too...too...boring. You're such a church boy and that's not what I want right now, maybe later after I've lived a little but not right now. I hope you can understand that," Imani said, folding her arms across her chest as an indication the topic wasn't up for further discussion.

"Was that Gregory?" For some reason that was the only question Darrel could think to ask in that moment.

"What difference does that make? You know what, I'll answer your question. Yes, that was him and before you ask, yes I've been seeing him," Imani said, now resting her hand on the doorknob.

Darrel remembered standing from the couch he had purchased and walking out the door without another question, he didn't even tell her good-bye. All he could think about in that moment was getting out of her presence and the words of wisdom his mother had poured into him for so many years.

"Don't ever put your hands on a woman. I don't care what she does to you, don't you lift a finger to her. You walk away son. It's a lot easier to heal from walking away than putting your hands on her and fighting to get your character back." The words of his mother played over and over in his mind as he made his way to the parking lot.

The entire walk to the car Darrel fought the vision that was prominent in his head of going back and slapping the taste out of Imani's mouth, but then he would never be able to look his mother in the face if he did.

When Darrel made it to his car, he sat there for several minutes processing what had taken place. He desperately needed to talk to someone about what just took place, but he wasn't sure who he could trust with the raw emotions he was feeling. He wasn't ready to have this conversation with his mother. Although she meant well, she sometimes got the 'L' words mixed up. She didn't know when he just needed her to listen instead of lecture on what he should have done.

"Pop's, you busy?" He needed a man to talk to.

"Not too busy for my boy. What's up son?" His dad could always sense something in his voice.

Darrel remembered telling his dad everything, from the first time he paid Imani's bills to the disrespectful way she broke up with him. He was so full of emotions that he allowed himself to be completely vulnerable with his dad by letting the tears he cried speak for him when words wouldn't come.

Darrel remembered how supportive his dad was in that moment. His dad shared with him the love tragedies he himself had experienced prior to meeting his mother. He reassured Darrel that the woman God had for him was out there and the key to finding her would be truly forgiving Imani.

"I'm not saying it will be easy, but I am saying it's a must. If you don't forgive her, you will never be able to fully heal and fully love another woman again son," Darrel remembered being happy he called his dad instead of his mother, as the conversation would have gone in another direction.

It took him a while to heal but he did it. He even treated Imani as if she did nothing wrong to him. He knew her apology a year after the breakup helped in his healing process. She went on to marry Gregory but from what he had been told, she wasn't happy. Deep down inside he had to admit he was happy to know she wasn't completely happy but at the same time wished her the best. After all, he knew a true Christian wouldn't take joy in someone else's brokenness.

THIRTY-FOUR

Darrel decided that thoughts of how Imani had done him shouldn't be on his mind as he headed to pick up his true soul mate. It only served as a reminder of just how silly he once was as a young man. Imani may have left his wallet and confidence broke with all of her name brand demands and head games, but she didn't break his desire to love again.

Getting over her made it easy for him to see Layla and know she was nothing like Imani. Imani may have been super model material but a far cry from wife material. Her attitude was worse than what the trash man picked up five days a week, and he often wondered how he put up with it so long. She had him feeling like he was nothing when it was all said and done but he was raised better than that. He knew he had to be like the prodigal son and come to himself. Once he did that, along with getting busy in his local church, he felt his confidence slowly resurface.

Darrel was ready to put all of that behind him and start a new life with Layla. She had past the materialistic test and the self-centered test that both he and his mother had given her. He was thankful for her unconditional love and he intended on proving that their first night on the boat.

The two lovebirds arrived at the hotel they would stay overnight at that evening. They settled in and went back out for dinner. After dinner they did a little sightseeing and a little shopping. They decided to call it a night a little after 11:00 p.m. Darrel wasn't sure how he would handle the sleeping arrangements. Layla smelled so good to him and he was hoping he could control himself with her lying in the other bed that was next to his. To his surprise there was no temptation but rather something he hadn't felt with another woman in a long time, peace. He figured their prayer made that possible.

"Lord, we thank You for safe travel and another opportunity to be together. We thank You for thinking enough of us to place us together at Your appointed time. We ask that You continue to guide our decisions and have a mind to be in Your perfect will. We will continue to give You all the glory, honor and praise. Amen." Darrel heard Layla pray.

Hearing Layla pray made her even sexier to him. Her growth as a woman of God made him fall even more in love with her.

That next morning, they got up got dressed and over breakfast they talked about what they would do once on the boat. Once they finished breakfast they checked out the hotel and headed to the airport. Darrel parked his car in the long-term parking lot before they got on the shuttle that would take them to the boat. Once they arrived, they were both excited as they laid eyes on the huge boat for the first time. Neither had been on a cruise before and was happy they were experiencing it for the first time together.

At check in, Darrel gave the attendant his Black American Express Card and their bags. Once on the boat they stopped, took pictures, and headed towards many of the shops that were on the boat. They took more pictures with their camera and made plans for what they would do for the remainder of the week. The options were endless, and they wanted to fit in as much as they could. The two sat on the balcony outside of their room and enjoyed the sight of the beautiful ocean. The scenery was breathtaking, and Darrel was so glad he was experiencing the view with a woman who deserved it. They took pictures and talked about everything under the sun. Darrel felt like they were closer than ever before, and it made his plans perfect timing.

They stayed out on the deck until it was time to get ready for dinner. This was the night Darrel planned to propose and everything had to be perfect. He figured this night would either break or make the rest of their trip, either way he was ready to find out. He had two surprises for Layla; he was sure she would like one of them but he wasn't sure about the other.

After a wonderful dinner, the waiter asked if they were ready for dessert. After they said yes and placed their order, he asked her how she was enjoying the trip so far.

"Baby it has been absolutely great so far," Layla answered.

They were sitting towards the front of the large dinning room.

"That's good to know," Darrel said, signaling to the waiter.

"I know I don't say it often, but I really do thank God for you. You came into my life just when I was about to give up on love," Layla said, fighting back tears.

Darrel decided not to speak but let her keep talking as out the corner of his eye saw the waiter heading toward their table. When the waiter reached the table, he placed a large white silver covered plate in front of them both. Darrel hurriedly removed his cover to show the cheesecake with strawberries he ordered.

"That looks delicious baby. Let me get myself together so we can enjoy our dessert. I know you don't want to deal with a cry baby every night at dinner," Layla said, chuckling, using the linen napkin to dab her eyes and nose.

"You're just fine, baby. You know you can be who you are with me. Besides, I love the cry baby in you," Darrel said, chuckling along with her before taking a small bite of his dessert.

When Layla removed the cover from the plate, there was a large note with a small box on the plate instead of the cheesecake she was looking for.

Layla briefly looked over at Darrel before reading the note to herself.

You showed me how to love again and for that I'm grateful. I want to love you for a lifetime. Will you continue on the journey as my wife?

Layla looked over at him with a fresh set of tears in her eyes before speaking.

"Are you sure you want to be with *me* for the rest of your life? I don't believe in divorce sir," Layla said, quietly laughing in between her tears.

"Layla, I've never been more sure of anything in my life. God made you just for me girl and I refuse to let you get away," Darrel said, reaching over to pick up the ring before standing.

"Yes. I would be honored to be your wife," Layla said, holding her hand out to receive her ring.

As the two hugged, their family clapped as they moved in closer to them. Layla was genuinely surprised to see her parents, brother, sister-in-law and niece coming toward her. Darrel had worked overtime making the arrangements to make sure everyone was there to celebrate the next step in their life. His father shook his hand and his mother gave him the longest hug as tears ran down her face. His brother and sister, along with their families, were there to wish him well, too.

They all celebrated the engagement into the wee hours of the morning. As the two made their way to the room, they agreed there would still be no sex before they got married. They didn't want to do anything that would jeopardize what God was doing in their life.

Right before they got to their room, there was a couple walking towards them. Layla stopped in her tracks and looked as if she saw a ghost.

"What is it baby?" Darrel asked, as he held her around her shoulders.

"I would have to see him on the happiest day of my life." Darrel heard Layla say under her breath.

"See who baby?" Darrel asked, confused.

"Kelvin, my ex," Layla said, sadness in her tone.

Darrel wasn't sure how he should feel about this revelation. Knowing the history between Layla and Kelvin would this cause her to have a change of heart or had she truly moved on and ready to start a new life with him. Refusing to dwell on the negative possibilities or let Layla feel conflicted, he reassured her he was the one for her.

"I believe this is God's way of letting you know that you're finally free, lady," Darrel said to her while hugging her tight.

As Layla returned the inviting hug, Darrel's mind quickly went back to his past relationship history and now struggled to convince himself the words he just spoke were actually true.

Levi

THIRTY-FIVE

It was a month after Levi finally confirmed to Keitha that he was planning to get married and she was in full swing of making his life miserable. Her demands for more money while giving him less time with his daughter had started to grow out of control. He had complied with almost every outlandish request she came up with but refused the one where she demanded he spend time with TaShari at her home. He knew if he complied it had the potential to cause problems he wasn't prepared to handle.

So far he had been successful in keeping Keitha's demands hush-hush from Whitney but wasn't sure how much longer he could keep it up. It had taken him a few months to convince her to start planning the wedding and he didn't want to give her any reason not to continue. Between Keitha's Facebook posts and Instagram snapshots, he knew it wouldn't be long before Whitney picked up on the pot of mess Keitha had been working overtime to stir up. He had decided to bite the bullet and clue Whitney in on some of the drama that was going on with his daughter's mother over dinner.

"I really don't feel like going out to dinner tonight. It is the last week of school and I have a lot of lose ends to close out. Can we wait until the weekend?" Levi heard Whitney ask him.

He really didn't want to wait a second longer especially not two days.

"Babe, I really need to talk to you about something," Levi said, looking at his watch.

"Well, stop by my place around seven and we can talk then. I have to go, honey," He heard Whitney say before hanging up the phone.

Levi placed his cell phone on top of his desk and began clearing the contracts from his desk. He recently started his own entertainment promotion business a few weeks' prior and business was starting to slowly trickle in. He had started working on obtaining the necessary licenses and permits in order to get the business up and going a few months ago and couldn't believe how quickly everything was coming together. He had not told Whitney about this either. His goal was to tell her after he had a return on his investment. He knew she would wonder if she was the reason he depleted his savings and partnered with Craig in order to prove he could really take care of her.

Levi was confident the pink elephant in the room would no longer be a guest if his business continued to pick up. He had decided to go for broke by investing in a dream he had on the back burner since before his daughter was born. He had already made one fourth of his investment back and he was only two weeks in.

Craig had a big part in helping him bring in celebrity talent. Since Craig was a professional athlete, he still had major connection to the industry and was more than happy to put Levi in contact with them. Levi had handled security at his club for years and Craig was impressed with what he saw and was willing to take a chance on him. If things continue to go the way they had been, he should have his money back and then some in time for the wedding. He had worked hard on making all the right connections within the city of Austin, and it was starting to pay off. Social media had done wonders in promoting his business and had saved him a lot of money on his marketing budget.

Levi had successfully negotiated contracts for three major celebrity appearances. After sealing the deal, he found out three other entertainment firms had been courting the same contracts but could never get them to commit. He was able to underbid his competitors since he didn't have a large overhead yet. He figured by the time the need arose for that, he would have enough long-standing clientele that he could start charging the new ones a little more.

Levi's office consisted of two employees, his receptionist Sherri, and Alex, who was his property manager. His receptionist worked five days a week, four hours a day while his property manager was on call. Sherri was a full-time college student and was satisfied with the ten dollars an hour he paid her. He allowed her to do homework while at work as long as the office business was taken care of first. She actually decorated the office for him and he was pleased with the outcome. The modest office had just enough space for one large office space and two smaller spaces, a conference room, and a receptionist area. It was small compared to some of his competitors but just big enough to make him a contender. Craig occupied the next to the biggest office periodically, which left one free for a possible future employee.

It was 5:30 pm and Levi had just set the alarm on his building and was heading home to take a shower. Since the engagement, he hadn't been taking as many showers or staying overnight at Whitney's place as much as he had in the past. At her request, she told him he needed to think about staying at his place more often.

"Aren't we going backwards?" Levi recalled saying.

"Why? Because I keep telling you no?"

"Well, yes. I think we should be practically living together by now."

"Because you put a ring on it?" Levi remembered her holding her hand up and wiggling the finger that held the diamond he had placed on it.

"Yes. Do you know how much money I spent on that ring? That alone should allow me to take as many showers and stay as many nights as I want."

"And if I allow that you will get lazy and we will never make it down the aisle," Levi remembered Whitney saying as she handed him the last duffle bag containing his personal items she had packed.

He remembered debating the subject with her for at least another hour. Part of him thought she may have another man taking up her time, but his common sense quickly dispelled that crazy thought. He knew she was a good girl and would not step out on him. He believed her when she told him she didn't want to curse their upcoming nuptials.

"I want to do things a little differently. I want us to have the same kind of love my aunt and uncle have. I want us to go the distance, babe," Levi recalled her saying right before kissing him softly on his lips.

He couldn't do anything but respect what she said to him that night. It took a while, along with a lot of self-discipline, to comply but he was doing better. There was no way he could take all the credit. Levi knew what was helping him with that--his newfound relationship with Christianity, and he was thankful.

If someone asked him a few years ago about anything having to do with religion, he would have not-so-politely closed the door in their face. He didn't want anything to do with the subject and didn't have a problem letting you know. Luckily for him, one of his clients asked him to meet at their church to go over the proposal he had sent them. They were preparing for a huge concert and had just secured a national gospel recording artist. When he arrived at the church, it was during one of the mid-week services and Levi liked what he heard. The praise and worship was something he had never heard before and the testimonies from different ones about all they had made it through did something to him. He was hooked and started visiting the church regularly. He had been thinking about joining but wasn't sure if he should wait so that he and Whitney could join together.

Levi was never raised in church but always had a curiosity about it. He believed there was a God but just wasn't sure how to seek Him. He had been going to Mt Mills for the past two weeks without Whitney and was enjoying what he received during each visit. He was learning about the Bible and how it tied back to himself and how he lived his life. This was something he was excited about but wondered how receptive Whitney would be to it, especially since he had refused to go to church with her the entire time they were together.

His refusal to grow with her spiritually used to be the source of many of their arguments until one day she had stopped asking. He also noticed that she had started drinking more wine around that time too, and her new job wasn't helping her put the bottle down either. He knew that if she got wind of the drama he had going on with his daughter's mother, there would be no hope of her letting go of the bottle anytime soon. Levi knew he had to have the conversation this evening or the chances would be next to impossible of keeping Whitney from finding out by way of someone else. If that did happen, he knew he would be calling on the Lord and it wouldn't be due to him hearing a powerful message from the preacher.

THIRTY-SIX

By the time Levi arrived at Whitney's place, he had received six missed calls from Keitha and she was calling back again. He really didn't want to talk to her again, especially while in the presence of Whitney. All he was focused on was informing his fiancé that his daughter's mother had seemingly lost her mind over their upcoming wedding, and it was looking like the only way to help her find it was to take her back to court. He knew the first thing Whitney would think about was the amount of money it would cost, and most likely cause her to have second thoughts about permanently attaching herself to him as his wife. It seemed the more things he had going good for himself, the more new things started falling apart. When he reached Whitney's door he decided to put his phone on silent.

"Hey you. How is my lovely doing this evening?" Levi asked Whitney after she answered the door.

He kissed her gently on the cheek and handed her a dozen red roses.

"Aw, thank you, babe. I'm good now that you've finally arrived. What took you so long?" Whitney asked smelling the roses as she headed towards the kitchen.

"I had an important call come through and it took a little longer than I thought it would," Levi answered.

Technically, he wasn't lying. He had received a call from his ministry leader at the church, but he also received a call from Keitha. After the initial call with her he had decided to ignore the rest of her calls for the remaining of the evening.

"Don't you hate it when that happens, especially when you have things to do?" Levi heard her say to him.

He decided to change the subject.

"So, what did you decide for dinner? Are you going to let me take you out on the town tonight?" Levi asked, now standing in the kitchen with her.

He studied her body language wondering if she was really in a better mood than she was when he spoke to her earlier or if she was just acting, something she had recently mastered.

"Sure, I think I need to get out of the house for a little bit. Might help me clear my mind a little," Whitney said, hugging him around the neck and resting her head in his chest.

This loving gesture put a smile on Levi's face and also put him at ease.

"Sounds like a plan. Where would my lovely like to eat?" He squeezed her a little tighter in his arms.

"You know what, I have a taste for pancakes from IHOP."

"Cool with me," Levi said, releasing her from his embrace.

"Let me get my shoes and my purse and I will meet you downstairs," Whitney said, before heading towards her room.

Levi smiled and walked out the front door. As he walked towards his car, he couldn't believe his eyes. Keitha was standing next to his car with a pink overnight bag and his daughter. He was so focused on them that he didn't notice her sister and best friend parked in the car next to his.

"What are you doing here?" Levi asked, doing his best not to yell in front of his daughter.

"What do you mean what am I doing here? I told you on the phone what I wanted but you hung up on me," Keitha said, one hand on her hip.

"And I told you I couldn't do it tonight. I told you my sister would do it since you claimed you couldn't put off what you had going on until tomorrow," Levi said, doing his best to stay calm.

He already knew by way of Instagram that she was going to the club. Why she insisted on going on a Wednesday night was beyond his understanding, but he knew if he searched social media hard enough he would be able to find out.

"And I told you it's not her job to keep *our* daughter," Keitha responded, shifting her weight to her right hip.

Levi was boiling on the inside by this point and luckily he noticed the spectators parked next to him.

"Baby girl, why don't you go get in the car with your auntie while I talk to mommy," Levi said, leaning down and kissing is daughter.

"She don't need to go get in the car. The bottom line is she is staying here with you and the Misses while I go take care of some business," Keitha said, holding out his daughter's pink bag.

"I don't have time to play these games with you, Keitha," Levi said, not taking the bag.

"Ain't nobody playing games here, boo boo, but you. I asked you if you was sure this was what you wanted and you gave me my answer when you hung up in my face. So, I suggest you take this bag and your daughter until I come to get her tomorrow evening," Keitha was giving him a look as if she was hoping he would escalate the issue further than it already was.

"What is going on, Levi?" He had completely forgotten about Whitney.

"Babe…nothing…please…can you wait for me in the house? I will be up there in a minute," Levi said, walking over and grabbing her by the hand.

He was doing his best to reassure her she had nothing to be worried about.

"Yes, please go back upstairs so I can finish talking to *my* daughter's father," Keitha popped off which caught Levi and Whitney off guard.

"Excuse me?" Whitney asked, now walking towards Keitha in an effort to make sure she heard her right.

"Baby, please let me handle this. You have too much to lose to get caught up with *her*," Levi said, gently holding Whitney by her arm.

He noticed she stood still for a few moments before speaking.

"Shari, you want to come upstairs with me? I'm sure I have some of your favorite cookies and ice cream," Whitney said genuinely smiling at his daughter.

When TaShari happily ran towards Whitney calling her 'momma Whit' while hugging her he knew that made Keitha mad. He could see the change in her attitude and confidence. He seized the moment by grabbing the bag from her and gave it to Whitney.

"We will be upstairs waiting on you, honey," Whitney said, before giving him a gentle kiss and totally ignoring Keitha as she and Shari headed back towards the apartment.

Keitha lunged towards Whitney but Levi jumped in the way.

"We are not doing this today. You got what you wanted, didn't you? You demanded I keep my daughter tonight, so what is the problem? Your plan to cause problems for me and my soon to be wife didn't work?" Levi said, looking her in the face.

"It's not fair! It was supposed to be me, not her!" Keitha said at the top of her lungs, all her cool gone.

"I think it's time for you to leave before you're made to leave. I will have *our* daughter ready for you to pick her up by six thirty tomorrow evening as you requested. I need you to be on time as I have a busy weekend planned and I don't want any foolishness from you," Levi said, walking away before allowing her to respond.

Although he did care about the wellbeing of the woman who was now calling him every name in the book, his priorities were the people inside the apartment waiting on him. He was willing to do whatever it took to keep Whitney and TaShari safe and happy, and if that meant leaving Keitha on the sidewalk screaming at the top of her lungs, so be it.

L. A. Logan

THIRTY-SEVEN

Levi headed back to the apartment and did his best to clear his mind in anticipation of the conversation he had to have with Whitney. He knew Whitney had to be upset and he couldn't blame her. He was upset at Keitha's total disregard for their time and space. If the situation were in reverse, he wasn't sure he could have had as much restraint as Whitney did. He was sure the National Guard would've been called in after he got done.

He decided to call his boy Darrel and get his buy in on what he should do. He and Darrel had become close friends over the past year and was a good example of a family man.

"She did what? Man, you need to handle your business. Take her ghetto fabulous behind back to court," Levi heard his friend say.

"I keep thinking about it but she broke my pockets the last time I did that. I'm just now getting my business off the ground and trying to give my girl her dream wedding. I can't afford to be dealing with Keitha and her craziness right now," Levi said, now sitting on one of the four benches in the playground area.

"I can understand that, but you need to look at it this way, either way it go, it's going to cost you. The question is when. If I were you, I would keep it one hundred with Whitney, handle your business with Keitha and that way, you can start your marriage off right. The last thing you want to do is have Whitney walk away from you, my dude. She has no drama in her life, especially no kid drama so I take my hat off to her that she has been as cool about the situation as she has been. You know what R. Kelly said," Darrel was now laughing.

"And what's that, dude?"

"When a woman's fed up. And I know you don't want to lose a *real* woman behind a bird," Darrel said.

Both men laughed as they continued to talk for another ten minutes. Levi felt better after talking to Darrel and he had to admit, he had some solid points. It took Levi a long time to get Whitney to even start planning the wedding, and the last thing he wanted to do was ask her to stop so he could afford to take care of more drama his daughter's mother was causing him.

The best he could hope for was to explain the evening's events away and take Whitney to Dallas for a long weekend to attend her favorite authors, Michele Stimpson and Tiffany L Warren's annual book fest, like they had been planning to do for the past three months. He could only pray that Keitha would keep her word and pick TaShari up on tomorrow evening, so he could prepare to leave town the following morning. He knew

his sister would not be able to help him out if she did flake on him and he would be forced to cancel the trip.

Levi wasn't in the door five minutes before she asked to speak to him in her bedroom. He was prepared for almost anything she had to say except if she wanted to call off their relationship. That was something he refused to accept and was willing to do almost anything to prevent that from happening.

"I know, it was totally disrespectful, and I have addressed it with her," Levi said, in between every ten words Whitney said as she vividly expressed how upset she was.

"And what kind of mother puts their child through such foolishness? Who would just drop their child off with someone like they were...unwanted," She didn't say another word as the tears slowly fell.

Seeing Whitney like this upset Levi. He knew she was thinking back to her experience with her own parents and it made him mad that his actions were the reminder of such deep pain.

"Baby, please don't cry. Everything is going to be alright," Levi pulled her into his chest and did his best to console her as she quietly cried in his chest.

"We just have to pray for our bond to be tighter and against anything that tries to come against it," Whitney pulled away from him as soon as he finished his sentence.

"Pray, Levi?"

"Yes, pray. I know it's a shock to hear that come out of my mouth, but your guy is trying to get his act together spiritually, so I can be the whole man you need me to be," Levi said, with a slight smile.

He breathed a sigh of relief when he saw a smile appear on her face. They talked for a few more minutes and decided to finish the conversation when TaShari wasn't around. Whitney didn't want her to misunderstand the conversation as her being the problem when it was really her crazy mother.

They decided to order a pizza and stay in since TaShari had school the next morning. Whitney asked them to stay the night at her place since it was getting late. Levi watched

Whitney interact with TaShari and knew he couldn't have asked for a better woman. Whitney bathed TaShari, helped her in her pajamas and even read her a bedtime story. If he was an outsider looking in, he would think it was her biological daughter. This made him love her even the more.

Levi went into the living room to search for a song to play for Whitney. While scanning the music, he pulled his phone out to put it on the charger. He noticed he had a text message from Keitha.

I can't believe you have OUR daughter calling that woman momma! You need to make a choice, your daughter, or that woman but you won't have both and be happy. You think your child support is breaking you now, just wait. She won't want you after I get done with you.

Levi shook his head as he put his phone on the charger. He continued to search for a song that would describe his current mood. He decided on "A Fist Full of Tears" by Maxwell. This was the only song that could accurately explain how he was feeling when it came to the woman who was set on making his life miserable beyond imagination.

Levi was so caught up in the song that he didn't realize Whitney was now in the room.

"You must be upset to be thinking about fist and tears," Whitney said, gently touching him on the arm.

"I'm cool. Just clearing my head," Levi said, gesturing for her to sit down next to him on the couch.

They talked for a few moments before calling it a night. He slept in the spare bedroom with his daughter after saying a silent prayer, something he was getting used to doing.

That next morning, Whitney made them all breakfast before they headed out to start their day. The day was uneventful and seemingly went off without a hitch. Just as

Levi figured, Keitha didn't show up at the scheduled time and she wasn't answering her phone.

"So do I need to cancel my trip?" Levi heard Whitney ask him and he could tell by her tone she wasn't happy.

"No, even if I don't go, you're going," Levi said.

"I don't want to go by myself, Levi," Whitney was clearly upset at the thought.

"And you're not. Get your stuff together," Levi said.

It was Friday morning and Keitha was still missing in action. Levi decided to stop by her house, unannounced, and if push came to shove he would take TaShari to Dallas with them. He had family there who had already agreed to keep her whenever he needed while they were in town. He didn't want to disappoint Whitney. He knew she had been looking forward to this trip and kids weren't apart of the plans.

After they were all in the car, he headed over to Keitha's. Once there, he knocked on the door and waited twenty minutes, she either wasn't home or didn't open the door. They decided to stop at the gas station around the corner from her house to gas up. Levi was doing his best to reassure Whitney everything was going to be all right and they would still be able to do everything that was on her list.

"Isn't that your baby momma right there?" Levi looked in the direction Whitney was pointing.

It was Keitha walking up to the door of the store. Levi left the car parked at the gas pump and walked towards the entrance of the store. He walked in the store and found Keitha by the soft drinks.

"What are you doing here?" she asked.

"Getting gas. What are you doing here?"

"I had to walk up here from my house. My car isn't working," Keitha was clearly not happy to see him based on the tone of her voice.

"Well, come on, I will give you a ride back to the house," he offered.

"No! I'm not getting in the car with you. I will meet you back at my house," Keitha walked towards the entrance of the store, changing her mind about whatever purchase she was going to make.

"I don't want my daughter walking in this heat. I will drop both of you off at your house. I have somewhere I need to be," Levi said following behind her.

Once outside they began to exchange heated words. Levi knew his ex all too well and he knew she didn't want to walk to the mailbox to get her mail, let alone to the store. He decided to survey the small parking lot and saw her sister and best friend parked a few stalls down. He noticed Keitha was dressed up like she was going somewhere. He motioned for Whitney to send TaShari to him.

"What are you doing? You're seriously going to make us walk in the heat?" Keitha asked.

"No, your sister is right there. I told you I had something to do this weekend," Levi said.

He picked TaShari up and gave her a kiss and told her he would pick her up on Tuesday and she could stay the whole week with him. She hugged her daddy and grabbed hold of her mom's hand. As Levi walked back towards his car without saying another word to Keitha, she screamed several not so pleasant words to him from across the parking lot. She cared not about the attention she was drawing to them.

Once in the car, he began to explain to Whitney what happened.

"Baby, it looks like TaShari is crying," Whitney informed him.

The sight broke his heart but the next words out of Whitney's mouth made it better.

"Go get your baby from that ignorant woman. She can come with us."

"Are you sure?" Levi asked.

"I don't want you to have to choose between me and your baby," Those were the only words she got out before he exited the car.

TaShari came to the car first and Whitney did her best to calm her down as she watched her parents argue back and forth about each other's parenting skills. A few minutes later, Levi got in the car and was clearly upset. Whitney did her best to calm him down. It took an hour or so before Levi was at a point to engage in conversation.

"Babe, I owe you the world. Thank you for being the bigger woman," Levi said, lifting her hand, and planting a kiss on it.

It took several seconds before Whitney spoke.

"You're more than welcome but I think you and I both know this current situation is not going to work. When we get back from Dallas, we need to talk about the direction our relationship is going in," Levi's heart stopped for what seemed like several minutes after digesting what Whitney had said.

He figured this weekend was going to make or break his relationship with Whitney and he had to make the best of it. He decided to respond with six simple words.

"Can I play something for you?" Before giving her a chance to respond he turned on "I Don't Care" by Raheem DaVaughn.

"Don't talk, just listen," Levi said picking up her hand once again, but this time he held on to it while giving his baby girl in the back seat a huge smile before speaking.

"No matter, what daddy loves you, baby girl, and nothing or nobody will change that."

About the Author

L. A. Logan has worked for a major insurance company since 1998. In her spare time she enjoys reading, traveling, working in her church's ministry, and spending time with family and friends.

She is also the founder of Empowering Women from Passion to Purpose. L. A. currently lives in Arkansas and is the mother of a daughter and son.

Made in the USA
Coppell, TX
20 January 2023

11438074R00128